LARIAT

A ROAD KILL MC NOVEL

VOLUME 6

New York Times Bestselling author
MARATA EROS

http://marataeroseroticaauthor.blogspot.com/

Marata Eros FB Fan Page: https://www.facebook.com/pages/
Marata-Eros/336334243087970

*Cover art by **Willsin Rowe***

*Editing suggestions provided by **Red Adept Editing.***

ISBN-10: 1981914897
ISBN-13: 9781981914890

WORKS BY TAMARA ROSE BLODGETT

The **BLOOD** Series
The **DEATH** Series
Shifter **ALPHA CLAIM**
The **REFLECTION** Series
The **SAVAGE** Series
Vampire **ALPHA CLAIM**

&

<u>**Marata Eros**</u>
A Terrible Love (***New York Times*** Best Seller)
A Brutal Tenderness
The Darkest Joy
Club Alpha
The **DARA NICHOLS** Series
The **DEMON** Series
The **DRUID** Series
Road Kill MC Serial
Shifter **ALPHA CLAIM**
The **SIREN** Series
The **TOKEN** Serial
Vampire **ALPHA CLAIM**
The **ZOE SCOTT** Series

Music that inspired me during the writing of LARIAT:

Call for You
by *The Side Project*

DEDICATION

For our brave veterans of the United States of America.
Thank you for fighting for our freedom.

God bless you.

1

ANGELA

Pro-bono. My life as public defender.

My forearms slide across the cheap laminate-surfaced table, and I clasp hands with the woman who sits across from me.

Crooked teeth peek through a genuine smile. Strings of hair clump together as she leans forward, biting a lip cut from the fists of her abuser.

Dead abuser.

Mini Dreyfus no longer has to live in fear that at any moment she'll suffer a contusion, cut, or broken bone. The dead can no longer maim.

She momentarily releases my hands and swipes at her striking brown eyes that are leaking down her cheeks. "I can't stay here, Miss Monroe."

"Angela," I correct for the hundredth time.

Mini nods, her smile watery and thin. "Prison is its own thing. I'm unprotected here too."

I refrain from biting my own lip. This is the problem. Mini murdered her husband, a type of passive self-defense.

To me and many others, the x-rays documenting the years of abuse are enough to justify her actions. Mini Dreyfus doesn't belong in a maximum-security prison. An hour, a day, any amount of time is too much in my humble opinion.

But beating a man while he sleeps with a solid hickory baseball bat brings pause, even to the most sympathetic. So now there will be a trial.

In the meantime, Mini is being held without bail.

"I shoulda waited until he was beatin on me before I caved in his skull."

I nodded. Yes, she should have. But I'm Mini's attorney, and I can't outwardly agree with the violence.

However, I do on the inside.

I squeeze her hands, gently releasing my hold. "We can't hang onto regret."

She leans forward, lank and dirty hair forming a curtain between us as I move my face close to hers. "The only thing I regret is I didn't kill that fucker sooner."

Yes. Out loud, I say in a thready voice, "Be that as it may, we will have to put on a more neutral front for the trial." In other words, there can be no outward glee, no matter how much his death has made her giddy with profound relief.

Mini sits back, defiantly crossing her arms. "I don't know if I'm gonna live to see the trial, Angela."

Prison isn't for the faint of heart. It's not unheard of for a client who doesn't have any money to make bail—even if bail is set—get killed before the process is complete.

I'll ask the judge to set bail. It'll probably be denied, but he can only say no.

"Can ya talk to my cousin?" Mini asks suddenly.

My ears perk. "Cousin?" I frown. "What does your relative have to do with bail?"

She leans even closer, as close as her chains will allow, and I attempt to ignore the embedded grime in the creases of her neck. It's an effort to maintain my calm veneer, especially as Mini's life mirrors a familiarity that I don't want to see reflected back at me anymore.

"He's kinda rich. Haven't seen em since I was little, but he was good to me."

"You're saying that if I *can* get bail, he'll pay."

She shrugs. "I don't know. But he's a big deal SEAL, Navy man. Biker now, I hear. He'll have cash."

The cogs of my mind grind away. A man who was a hardened American assassin, that's now a biker gang member will just be *thrilled* with putting up a 100K for his wayward cousin.

I let the disbelief bleed into my carefully cultivated blank expression.

Mini squirms a little. "I know it's a long shot." She puts her head in her hands, threading her fingers through the loose strands. The chains clank against the metal perimeter of the table, stretching taut. "I got no one else. My folks are dead."

Mine too. I release a thoughtful breath.

She slowly raises her face. "He was my uncle's boy. Sometimes, when we were little, we were all each other had." Her fingers fall to her lap, the jangling metal loud in the enclosed space. She twists and untwists her hands over and over.

"Five minutes, Ms. Monroe."

I turn, only my profile visible to the guard. "Yes, thank you."

My face swivels back, and I prop my elbows on the table. "What happened to him?"

She lifts a shoulder and sniffs. "He moved outta state. Never heard from him again."

"Your parents died when?"

"Teenager. I started using after that. Uncle didn't want me."

I hike an eyebrow. I find it hard to believe that a family member who had a good son would have ignored a child in need. Something doesn't agree in this scenario. "Your uncle told you that?" I steeple my hands together underneath my chin as I watch every minute expression on her face.

4

Mini shakes her head. "No." Her breath shudders. "But he was contacted by a case worker and never came forward to, ya know, claim me." She casts her eyes down.

Fucker. "All right." I lightly rap my knuckles on the cheap laminate. "Give me his name, and I'll reach out." I lift a shoulder, and the fashionably fitted blazer I wear constrains the movement.

"Shane Dreyfus."

I feel my eyebrows rise, surprised they share the same last name.

Mini says, "Kept my own last name." Her chin lifts. "Arnie beat me harder for it. But it wasn't somethin I was gonna let him take—it was mine. Arnie didn't deserve it, for me to have his last name. He was less than a man."

I swiftly look down, thinking of another time, another place. A fine sheen of sweat springs above my upper lip, and my stomach rolls.

Settle down, Angel.

I employ deep-breathing exercises, one after another.

The guard lightly taps my shoulder, and I'm not expecting it. Unguarded.

I yelp.

He throws both hands up, retreating a step. "Whoa, sorry!"

My galloping heart slows as I gradually take charge of my emotions again.

Mini glares at him.

"It's fine." I clear my throat softly. "You startled me is all." I smooth my damp hands over my tight pencil skirt and stand.

Mini does too. Her dark eyes meet mine. So unusual in their large size, they take up the precious real estate of her face. They're so deep a brown that they swallow the pupil, appearing to float like smoldering rich pockets of earth within the delicate oval of her face. They're her most arresting feature.

Though the faded bruises beneath them are also noteworthy.

I nod, turning my attention to Mini. "I will do my best." I stretch my fingertips, touching her arm. "What biker gang does he belong to?"

Mini cocks her head, obviously trying to remember. "You're assuming that you can get me bail."

Our eyes lock again. Mine are a very light green with gold mixed in. Hers are like a night sky that never sees daylight.

"I am." I don't tell Mini I usually get what I want. I don't leave myself options for failure.

Once I have options, that is.

"Thank you, Miss Monroe."

"Angela." I smile, and it reaches my eyes, crinkling the corners. "The gang?" I prompt her.

Mini shakes her head. "Not sure. Just know he's MC."

MC?

Then a guard is leading her away. I watch her go, in her bright, hazard-orange prison outfit. She looks so small, like a stolen flower.

Wilted.

I've got my work cut out for me. I sigh and purposefully turn away.

I swipe my hands over my suit and straighten the lapels that lead to a single button beneath my breasts. I suck in a cleansing breath. Then another.

I will not be intimidated.

Yet, I am.

There's no amount of law school or cases won that will restore my confidence when faced with dangerous men.

Too many memories. Too many triggers firing off at once. I imagine the sensation is similar to being in the middle of a war zone.

I stare at the heavy wood door and will myself to open it.

I had put out the feelers to find Mini's cousin. I have only myself to blame if one of these men throws me down on the floor and has his way with me.

Hell, I almost invited it from the message I left with the right people.

I have something you want, I'd penned cryptically.

There was no way to find out where the Road Kill Motorcycle Club headquarters was located, which is the MC that Shane Dreyfus is associated with.

But Garcia's, a local Kent dive restaurant/bar, is the place where the cousin supposedly will meet me—in public.

Gripping the solid long metal bar of the restaurant door, I swing it wide and step inside.

Ambient noise immediately assails me as I notice a full-length mirror standing at attention to the right of the maître d' desk.

I glance at my reflection.

Luminescent eyes appear to glow, stranded in the midst of my hated freckled, fair skin. But my hair is jet black, belying that porcelain skin. A shocking contrast. Or so I've heard mentioned many times. The reality is, I was told I was ugly in my formative teen years, so my looks, whether good or bad, didn't receive a lot of introspection. I shake off cobwebs from the past. They stubbornly cling to the now.

What I *do* know is I'm smart. And determined.

I will get this cousin to fork over the money for the bail I managed to finagle from the reluctant judge—a judge who took ten minutes to pour over the graphic x-rays cataloging abuse too profound to ignore.

If I have to use whatever physical assets I have to assist in that bargaining chip, I will.

I run my hands over my black pencil skirt and drape the matching bolero jacket over my left arm. The citrine-colored blouse I chose matches my unusual eye color and has only three buttons. The first begins exactly where my cleavage starts.

I look as good as I can force myself to. I turn, scanning the noisy crowd. There isn't a spare seat in the house.

Except one.

A man with dark, closely cropped hair nurses a draft beer, casually spinning it on the highly polished bar top. His back is to me, and it's broad. The length of his legs suggests height, but God knows that never matters. I'm five feet ten in my stocking feet, and a man has to be six feet two before I notice his height.

It's the leather vest covered in patches that gives me the first clue that he's my man, or maybe it's the Road Kill MC scrolling across his back at the leather vest's center.

My lips curl, and I begin to walk toward him, but then I pause, just staring. The white noise of voices, clinking ice, and low music struggle around me like a pillowy cushion of sound I refuse to absorb.

There is something different about him, some enigmatic element that sets him sharply apart from the other patrons.

I continue to gauge that unique sensation, unhappy with my inability to identify what that piece of mystery is.

Then it hits me.

He is the only patron who appears causal but is not. I have never witnessed another human being who has such an innate talent for not just occupying a space, but making it come alive. The very air seems to vibrate with energy.

His energy.

The people who sit near to who I assume is Shane Dreyfus almost appear to lean away, as if they've gotten too close to the sun and are libel to be burnt.

His potential for danger is an aura I recognize immediately, and I'm instantly glad I chose this place instead of somewhere more private.

Of course, my background has taught me caution, and I employ that now. Every sense and instinct come alive as I prowl toward this lowlife biker.

I remind myself that Shane Dreyfus served our country then just as easily dismiss the notion. I'm not some young girl who'll get doe-eyed by a rough and tough ex-Navy SEAL.

I'm almost twenty-seven years old. And I feel as though I've lived two lifetimes to get to where I am now, to be who I am.

I will do what I must for Mini.

When I'm about five feet away, he turns, legs apart in a casual spread, and my eyes take him in up close.

Rugged. That's the word to describe Shane Dreyfus. Scuffed black, deeply tread, lace-up boots are hidden under dark denims that climb his muscular legs and continue over an impressive package. His waist is narrow but not waspy like the effeminate male models that are so popular right now. His strong hands loosely cradle the nearly finished beer, and broad shoulders hold a thick neck that sports an inky black anchor at its side, about the size of a quarter. His jaw is strong and square, a deep cleft in its middle.

When my gaze reaches his face, I find it holding a smirk. But the eyes—oh my God—they're Mini's. Coal black, they gaze unflinchingly back at me.

"Like what you see, sweet thing?" He tilts his head back, taking a swallow of his beer, and a lick of foam laces his upper lip. Those dark eyes eat the edges of my vision as his throat works the swallow.

I have an insane urge to kiss the foam off. The compulsion is so overwhelming, I hide behind a derisive laugh while I recover.

Shane Dreyfus frowns at my obvious lack of interest.

He's probably five feet six, I console myself. And in my two-inch heels, I will look down my nose and intimidate him into shooting dollar bills out of his ass.

I volley a hard smirk back. "Hardly," I reply in a cool purr. "Just enjoying the view."

His eyes tighten at my icy drawl.

A man to his left moves in as though to take the empty seat, and Dreyfus shoots him a look. "Fuck off."

The man backs away, hands raised. "Sorry, man, thought you were leaving."

Shane Dreyfus silently stares holes through him.

He scuttles away.

Poor thing. My smile broadens.

He turns his attention back to me. "You Angela Monroe?" He empties his beer and sets it hard on the bar top.

"I am."

I let the silence roll out, not bothering to fill it. Doing so is an alarmingly effective technique for destabilizing those I wish to manipulate.

Dreyfus lets the verbal stand off go, staring at me. His perusal mirrors the one I just gave him.

I'm sure he'll linger over the tight skirt, the hint of small but perfect breasts offered at the *V* of my golden-green blouse. But he doesn't pause at the obvious triangle that marks me as female.

He stares into my eyes. Deeply.

It's more disconcerting than if he'd just leered at all my obvious parts.

After two full minutes pass, he says, "Let's get out of here." He licks the foam from his upper lip.

My breath stills for a heartbeat at the gesture, and I shake my head. *No way.* This combustible chemistry is not going to be taken elsewhere. "Absolutely not. I chose this place because I'm safe here. And my safety comes first, Mr. Dreyfus."

His smirk is back, and he beats his knuckles with a sharp tap on the bar. The bartender races to where he sits. "Lady looks thirsty," he semi-growls at the bartender.

Wide, frightened eyes find me.

"Do you have UV?" I ask.

He nods rapidly.

"I'll take that with lemonade."

Dreyfus's smirk widens to a brilliant smile, flattening the sexy dimple on his chin, and he sweeps a palm toward the open stool.

I walk toward him, and he stands. He looms over me.

He's not five feet anything. He's six feet four if he's an inch.

"You're very tall, Mr. Dreyfus." I want to kick myself. Is that all I can say? I mean, I'm known as the golden tongue. And I mention height? My brains have clearly slipped out of my ears.

"So are you. And it's Lariat. That other name is just on paper."

He sticks out a hand, and I shake. But it's more like being swallowed whole.

Danger oozes out of him. But somehow, he makes me feel safe.

And that's why I have to get what I need and get the hell out. There is no such thing as safe.

It's a fairy tale.

And those, I never believed.

2

LARIAT

Bitch is *hot*.

I don't sit with my back to an exit unless I can see it. My eyes are steady on the mirror in front of where I sit at the bar. Bottles of liquor have the optical illusion of suspended liquid jewels, obscuring my view but not so much that I need to face the exit. There are two points for escape from my vantage point. My eyes restlessly travel from one to the other.

I know every person in this bar. Not by name, but by potential.

Dangerous potential.

The instincts of being a Navy SEAL never leaves a man. Can't take the service out of a SEAL. It's part of my makeup. It doesn't matter that I ride now. I served. And in my own way, I continue to serve.

I was expecting some late forties broad with a secretary spread and a cheap poly suit to frump in and tell me whatever bullshit some asswipe has trumped up. And what the fuck is with the secrecy?

I didn't expect this—not her. How do I know this is Angela Monroe? Well, for one thing, she screams lawyer from head to heeled toe.

She wears a tight black suit in a place full of denim and T-shirts. She sticks out like a turd in a punch bowl.

Fine looking doesn't cover it, and I feast on the reflected view the mirrored wall provides.

I don't normally have a type of chick I go for. Giving a rueful shake of my head, I take that back. When it comes to sweet butts—the whores of the MC—I like em young, tight, and willing. Those are the prerequisites. Dumb is a bonus. I don't want *more*.

Thank Christ I haven't joined the fucking demented pussy parade like Noose, Snare, and Wring. Those fuck-nuts—they are bitch-i-*fied*. I'll count the pennies for Road Kill MC. Then I'll let some broad swallow a load of what I have, or better yet, unload in her sweet hole.

Yeah. *That's* my style, not this committing bullshit. But god *damn* if this chick doesn't give me an insta-hard-on.

Why?

I would say it's the sizzling body I can see from the slim reflection offered by the mirror facing the crowded bar. But I've had hot. I would say that my reaction is because she has a vagina—but so do the three billion other chicks on this blue marble. I scrape a palm over the two-day stubble my jaw holds, puzzled.

Angela Monroe moves as if she owns the space she's in. She parts the crowd without saying excuse me, fuck off—whatever. People just move out of her way.

And she's got legs that go on for miles.

I know when she's made me. She stops her forward motion. People swirl around her, and I will them to move so I can continue to watch her while she's unaware she has an audience.

When she's a few feet away, I spin the stool around to face her.

I take a swig of beer to hide my reaction, mentally flogging my semi-boner into compliance.

Angela Monroe is gorgeous up close. Skin like fucking carved ivory with a smattering of freckles over the bridge of her nose. Jet black hair tops it off.

But the eyes...Her eyes are like fucking jewels embedded in her face. On a chick, I usually just notice the goods—T and A. But not on her.

She's delicate. I meet her confident gaze, which borders on defiance.

Her eyes are hard. Angela Monroe has been through a few things. Not good things, if I'm any judge. And I am.

Like recognizes like.

"Like what you see, sweet thing?" I ask to cover my tenseness before taking a gulp of brew.

Her lips curl. "Hardly." Then she tilts her head, studying me for a second as if I'm a really interesting bug. "Just enjoying the view."

Really? Well fuck *me.*

She doesn't play around. I like it. But I want to know why we're having this little soiree more.

Just as I'm ready to question our meeting, a guy tries to take the seat I was saving for her and momentarily interrupts my view.

Douche. "Fuck off." I give him my typical *I mean business* stare, and he takes off like a spider after a fly.

I turn my attention back to Angela. Maybe I can get laid if I play my cards right *and* get whatever she needs to tell me out of her. Two birds with one stone. I look her over again. Maybe she's out of my league.

"You Angela Monroe?" I have to confirm it. I figure she's the real thing, but I'm thorough.

"I am." Then she says she's not safe leaving here with me.

She's right, but not for the reasons she's thinking.

I lick my lips, anticipating. Chicks dig bikers, lawlessness—even professional chicks. My eyes hood. "Let's get out of here."

Her face breaks into a grin, but it doesn't reach her eyes. The expression is a hard, shiny flash of teeth.

My eyes rove over her again. *Jesus.* I transfer my beer to my other hand.

Fine.

I make the right words and indicate the stool. I stand as she walks by, and something flusters the fuck out of her. I don't know at first what it is.

Then I slowly get it.

I'm tall. I mean, I'm used to being tall and don't give it fuck-on-ditty attention. But her reaction to my nearness tells me she's not used to being this near a man who's so much taller than her.

The tenseness in her body gives her away as she practically flinches to avoid the closeness. I frown. That kind of response tells me she's probably seen the business end of some fists.

Some fuck put hands on her.

It's one thing to enjoy a bitch. It's a whole fucking other to hurt her. Women weren't put on this Earth to fuck up. Men protect women. And the ones who don't need to have a quick end—or a painful slow one. Depends.

If it were up to me, it would be a knotted termination.

I miss doing that—taking care of shit up close and personal. Now I count beans for the club because I have a mind for figuring. I always have. I've figured every stage of my life, and I'm not bad on strategizing either.

I don't spend a shit-ton of time being slow. Life depends on making snap decisions, instinctual shit. Slow just gets a man dead.

Safety is not what I want Angela Monroe to worry about, that I'm just another fucker who beats women.

All this slides through my mind in seconds. What I do outwardly is take the heat down a notch.

I perch on the stool, and her shoulders relax, sinking a touch. I knew sitting would help.

Without looking away from her, I hit my knuckles on the bar, and the little weasel bartender who makes weak drinks scurries back.

She gives her order—something tooty-fruity. I snort. I don't meet a lot of females who like straight beer. It seems to offend.

I shoot a daggered glance at Smarmy—pretty sure he gets the hint. Bartending simp better put enough vodka in her drink for it to taste like one.

Angela Monroe slides onto the stool, letting an elegant ankle dangle just above the circular metal bar that encompasses the bottom of the stool's legs. She sits as though she's poised to take off.

"Shane Dreyfus," she murmurs.

My chin jerks up, and I realize I've been fantasizing about her leg, and shit a lot higher up.

I'm usually not this obvious.

"Call me Lariat."

She lifts a brow but doesn't comment, her lips tweaking in a secret smile.

Makes me wonder what she's thinking. I frown, breaking a long-standing internal tradition of *I don't give a shit.*

I prop an elbow on the bar as her drink comes. The bartender sets a tall, icy blue concoction in front of her with a skinny, bright red, plastic swizzle stick.

I spare him a dark glance. "Better not be weak, pal."

He looks at me, Adam's apple doing a throat dance. "No way."

I grunt and turn back to her.

"I'll get right to the point."

My dick nods when her sultry voice starts in. Timing sucks, but the fucker has a life of its own. I've never had a body part as uncooperative as my prick. I shift my weight, trying to subtly adjust the goods.

"The point would be good."

Her exhale is slightly irritated, and that pisses me right the fuck off.

I straighten. I'm mad because of my body's response and pissed because she acts like she's God's gift. "*I'm* here because of your fucked-up message, so say what you gotta say."

She nods, seemingly unfazed by my words. "I should have never come, but Mini assured me you were her only hope."

Her eyes pierce me, waiting for my response.

Shit. "Mini?" Man, I thought she was gone—dead. Dad told me before he bit it that he didn't know what happened to her. We figured she moved away, or hell, that she was dead.

I can't hide my excitement and concern. "Is she all right?" Dumb question. Why would she lawyer up if things were fucking *good*?

Angela sweeps an inky strand of hair that's come loose from some bun thing behind her ear.

I want to touch that soft tendril—badly. I want to feel if it's as silky as it looks. I try to shake off the urge.

We're talking about my cousin that I haven't seen in ten years, and I'm lusting over her lawyer.

I take another pull of beer from the icy bottle Smarmy brought, trying to calm my tits.

Angela laces her fingers together as if she's trying to work up to what she needs to tell me.

"What?" I bark, harsher than I meant the one word question to be.

But Ms. Monroe doesn't seem to be moved by my brashness.

"She is okay, but I'm trying to assure her safety. Get her out of a place she definitely doesn't belong in."

Her eyes have thawed, and I realize in that moment that she cares about Mini.

"Mini's in trouble," I say, guessing the obvious.

Angela nods. "She's in prison."

I laugh because I can't help it. I remember Mini as a snot-nosed little girl, following me around like a puppy. I was the big brother she never had. Then shit went south, and that was all she wrote. "Come on, ya gotta be joking." Even I can hear the thick disbelief in my voice.

"I'm an attorney."

I shrug. "Guess I have to believe you."

"Why else would I want to meet with you?"

Ouch. I give her the look, check out her tits, and raise my eyebrows.

"Please, spare me." She rolls her gorgeous golden-emerald eyes. "I wouldn't have sex with you if you paid me."

Now that just pisses me off. "Not your type?" I ask way fucking cooler than I feel.

She looks me over—really slowly, as though she's memorizing my pores. Her jewel-colored eyes rise to my face, and for a heart-stopping moment, I think she's going to say something utterly different than what she says next.

"No." She sighs. "I hate to burst your bubble, but this is not a sexing endeavor. Your cousin is in prison for aggravated murder, and bail is set at one hundred thousand. Having met you, I now understand that is beyond your means. As she mentioned, it was a long shot."

The lack of faith from Mini and from Miss Stuck-up Lawyer adds insult to injury.

Angela stands, running a hand over her skirt and lifting a small black purse onto her shoulder. She sighs and gives me a semi-disgusted look that she doesn't bother to hide. "Thank you for meeting with me, Lariat. You were our last hope." She removes some cash from her purse.

I snatch her wrist, feeling the fragile bones beneath my hand, and heat whips through me at the contact. My hard-on comes back full tilt.

Angela's eyes widen, and I know in that moment, she feels it too. Raw chemistry swamps us.

I might not be her type, but I'm *something*. Anything else is a bald-faced lie.

"I can."

She tries to yank her wrist away, and my hold tightens, easily keeping her.

Angela's smart so she stops struggling. "You can *what*?"

I lift a shoulder. *Fuck.* "Provide the bail."

Her surprised expression is satisfying as fuck—and just as insulting. Her fear is less satisfying, even though it's laced with excitement. "Let go of me." Her voice is low and careful.

"Sure." I release her wrist with a flourish, and she rubs it, though I know I didn't hurt her.

Angela's slim black brows fold together. "You can'?"

I nod. "Fuck yes. I might be rough around the edges, but I have the cash."

I sip more beer, even though I'm not in the mood to drink anymore.

Her cocktail sits nearly untouched. But at my proclamation, she lifts it to her lips and takes a sip.

I'm riveted by her mouth. Her lips are a deep raspberry red. I wonder if they really are that color or if it's carefully applied makeup.

I hate makeup. Smells like shit, and it's false advertising.

A small laugh escapes those kissable lips, spreading them over white teeth. "Yes, you're rough, all right."

We stare at each other over the rim of her glacial blue drink.

"You like rough?" I ask, and my next breath stalls out waiting for her response.

She takes another sip, and my eyes peg her lips again. My dick begins to throb.

Those crystalline golden eyes meet mine. "Yes."

Holy fuck.

"You make my dick hard, Ms. Monroe."

Her laugh is a throaty shout, and it's like music to my ears. "I'm afraid there's nothing I can do about that."

"Hell yes, there is."

Angela sets her drink on the bar again. She opens her purse and digs around for a few seconds then extracts a card. Carefully, she lays a ten-dollar bill under her half-finished drink.

She slides a glossy rectangle across the bar. Her card.

Am I being dismissed? *Fuck that.* Twice. "Are you telling me to fuck off?" I laugh, crossing my arms and refusing to touch the card.

A fine blush spreads across her cheekbones. It feels good to know I'm getting under her skin.

"I don't know what this is"—she flicks her finger between us—"but the focus needs to be on my client. Her safety."

"I got that figured, Angela. Business is through. Now we're talking about fucking it out."

She blinks, taking a step back, and I watch the pulse in the hollow of her throat flutter beneath skin so light it's nearly translucent. "I don't think I'll be your partner in that, Mr. Dreyfus."

I stand, and she holds her position.

The mutual *want* suffocates us like smoke.

"Please phone me on Monday morning so we can talk about capital. In fact, swing by my office before nine, and we'll hammer out the particulars."

Capital. Springing Mini. Yes. My eyes go to her mouth again.

I grip her shoulders, and a gasp slides out between her lips. Definitely natural color, I decide, inspecting her deep red lips close up.

I knead the small muscles where her shoulders meet her neck, and she bites back a groan. Her head sort of tilts backward.

"I'll see you Monday, but it's not gonna be about money." My eyes search her face, memorizing every contour. "I already said I'd pay. But now there's something else I want."

She jerks away from me and spins, walking toward the door without a backward glance.

I'll take care of my blood, and Ms. Monroe will take care of my libido.

Whether she realizes it or not.

3

ANGELA

Arrogant prick.

Fuck it out. Right. I don't care if he's hot. And that's some kind of magnetism I just walked away from.

I'm not an alley cat.

My palm slaps the entrance door to the restaurant. The drink Lariat bought for me is curdling like spoiled milk inside my stomach. He got me so fired up, I do the unthinkable and drop a habit I've clung to for almost a decade.

I don't take in my surroundings.

The cool air slaps me like an invisible hand as I step outside into deepening twilight. I shiver, the noise from the bar instantly silenced as the big door swings closed behind me.

My concealment permit allows me to carry a handgun, but the inconvenient location inside my handbag makes it a fumble if I really need to get it quickly.

Like now.

"Hey, bitch," a voice says from my left.

I react instantly, slamming my elbow backward into where I assume the largest part of where that threatening voice came from.

It's a wasted blow, but the element of surprise is important. A satisfying *oof* sound disseminates, and I take off, heels clicking on the pavement as I race to my car, hoping I bought myself time.

A hand latches on to the knot of hair at my nape, dragging me backward.

Didn't buy myself any time.

Reaching my arms up, I seek my assailant's eyeballs with my thumbs and scrape my nails against his jaw instead. I let myself fall, becoming dead weight in his hold, forcing him to let me go.

I land hard, one elbow taking the impact.

His foot finds my torso, kicking the wind out of me and bruising a rib.

I latch onto his foot as it retreats and yank.

He stumbles, and I swing my leg around, high heel sailing off, and nail his knee with my instep.

He howls, and I get to my hands and knees. My skirt is hiked up to my hips.

He reaches for me, and I recognize him.

I bite Tommy's arm because that's the closest weapon I have. He screams, trying to pull away, and I clamp my teeth down harder.

His other hand rises in a fist.

I roll, trying to avoid the punch, but he strikes my face. Stars burst in front of my vision. Tommy leans over, grabs the lapels of my jacket, and hikes me halfway off the ground.

"Nobody runs from me," Tommy growls as his foul breath bathes my face.

I slam my forehead into his.

He drops me, and my head cracks against the asphalt.

I lie on my back, momentarily stunned. My breath is well and truly stolen as I gaze at the light-polluted sky.

"Get the fuck away from her."

I know that voice. Groaning, I attempt to roll on my side, but nausea shoots up and out like a spewing fire hose. *Must've hurt myself with that graceless landing more than I thought.*

"This isn't your business," Tommy says.

I don't want to be in a compromising position with Shane Dreyfus—Lariat.

I wipe a shaky hand roughly over my mouth and glance up. *Too late.*

Tommy and Lariat are squaring off, and I manage to roll onto my ass. I notice my panties are flashing the parking lot, and I don't give a shit.

Tommy is lower than pond scum. He'll mess Lariat up, Navy SEAL or not. *Tough biker. Whatever.*

I open my mouth to tell Lariat to leave it alone as his fist flashes from what seems like behind his shoulder.

Tommy's head snaps back. He takes a lurching backward stagger and shakes his head. With a roar, he charges Lariat.

I scramble to my feet, sway with dizziness, and slap my hand on the door of my smart car. Pain electrifies my side where Tommy's shoe landed, and I gasp, holding a hand to my abused ribcage.

My eyes go wide. *What in the hell?* I think I'm seeing things.

Is that a knot rope?

The bulbous end of a double-knotted length of rope snaps at the end of Lariat's arm and smacks Tommy in the nose.

He drops to his knees, hands slapping the pavement.

Lariat ignores me as I attempt to hold myself up against the car.

He looks down at the fallen man. "Stay down."

"Can't." Tommy spits blood on the asphalt then begins to rise.

Lariat nods then kicks him in the head. The impact sends Tommy sprawling to a hard landing on his back. Still.

"Oh God." I flat palm my hands along my car as I walk to the back. I get to the hatchback and look down at Tommy.

My eyes go to Lariat, though I can't make them out very well in the crappy parking lot lighting. "You shouldn't have done that, Lariat," I manage to gasp out.

He snorts, stuffing the length of rope in his front pocket. Lariat takes an exaggerated look around, spinning with his muscular arms spread wide away from his body. Then he grins, letting his arms fall with a slap against his denim-clad thighs. "Ya see any other white knights coming to your rescue?"

Actually, no one was around but him and me. Tommy would have finished what he began if Lariat hadn't strolled along.

I knew it. He knew it.

My fingers tremble as I shove my disheveled hair behind my shoulder.

"Thank you," I whisper to my shoes.

"What?" he asks.

I look up, and he's cupping his ear. *God.*

I rotate my shoulders and bite my lip to stifle the pain. "Thank you," I repeat more loudly.

He smirks then frowns.

"What?" I ask, unable to read his expression.

"That dickhead get some licks in?"

I nod.

His eyes run down my body.

Oh my God. My skirt is bunched at my waist. I try to jerk the material down with the hand not pinned to the car.

"Love the view, but thinking you might not want Garcia's patrons gettin the whole show," Lariat says.

Or him. *Jesus.*

Nausea rolls through me again, and my vision swims. I clutch the side of my car as I try to hike down my wayward skirt. But it's tight for a reason—fashion not practicality. Once it's up, it's hard to get the thing down.

"Hey," Lariat says in a gentle voice.

I startle at his sudden nearness and hold up my palm. Instantly, I realize my mistake as I lose my balance and stagger backward. The sky tilts, and I feel myself falling.

Suddenly, strong arms that feel like flesh-covered steel encircle me, and my head tips forward against his chest. The world hasn't stopped spinning yet.

He smells good, like motor oil, spice, and male. My head rolls against his chest, my cheek coming to a stop over his strong heartbeat.

"Let me go," I manage, proud that my voice is only a little wispy.

"Fuck that."

I laugh, and a silent tear squeezes out of my eye.

"It's okay." I shoot out a tight breath. "Let me go, and I'll drive home."

"No." His voice is like smooth gravel rumbling against the inside of my skull.

"He'll wake up, and then our problems will really begin." I'm trying here, trying to help him.

Lariat seems stubborn.

"He doesn't know what problems are yet. I want to get you out of here and get some pesky questions answered."

That's not ideal.

I try to back away but can't move.

"You gonna upchuck again?"

Shame coats me. That's what every girl wants—a hot guy who she put in his place witnessing her most vile and mortifying moments. Yes. *A fantasy come true.*

"I don't think so." My fingers clutch at the smooth leather of his vest, hanging on for dear life.

"You're lucky."

Again, I don't think so. Having a mob thug assault me while trying to get a guy like Lariat to provide money for my client's bail and then rescuing me is *not* lucky.

"Used the club truck tonight. It's a hunk of shit, but it runs okay."

"What?" My brain is fuzzy when I really want to be clear—sharp.

Tommy moans from the ground.

Lariat scoops me into his arms.

"Put me down." More spinning.

"Nope." He strides to Tommy.

I have an inkling of what he might do and have a moment to say, "No!"

Then Lariat stomps his crotch.

Tommy's eyes spring open, and he bellows.

Lariat is grinding the heel of his black boot into Tommy's dick. "Calling card, dickhead. Leave. Chicks. Alone."

Lariat looks down at me, his eyes lingering on what I'm sure is a beautiful bruise forming on my cheek. "Especially this one," he adds with smooth menace.

Lariat uses Tommy crotch like a step stool and puts our full weight on it. Then he hops lightly off, using Tommy's pathetic pecker like a springboard.

Tommy shrieks, sitting straight up, his hands clutching his decimated crotch.

Oops.

Lariat chuckles, giving a nod of satisfaction. "Nice."

I cling to him, guessing what Tommy will eventually do when he recovers from Lariat's tap dance.

Lariat walks us to a late-model pickup truck. It's large and dented. It's layered in various stages of cancerous rust but looks as though it was red when it was new.

"My handbag," I say.

"Yup. On it." He presses me gently against the truck, hunts his keys out of his front vest pocket, inserts them, and the door opens.

Lariat slides me in the backseat, and I lie there, staring at the torn ceiling fabric inside the cab.

I hear his solid boot treads slap the road as he walks back to my tiny car. I sit up, just making him out as he plucks my purse off the asphalt. He eyeballs Tommy, who is still writhing and clutching his balls, and makes

34

his way to the truck, slipping inside as silently as a ghost.

He turns over the engine and backs out.

I grab the back of the bench seat and breathe through the pain, gazing out of a rear window that has a fine spiderweb fracture running through the glass.

Tommy is on his knees, which is where he said I would be someday when I was putting his boss away for life.

I hadn't believed him then, but I should have known he would try to make good on his threats. Still, it wasn't the first time I've been threatened, and it won't be the last.

I thought the gun would protect me, but it's only as good as my level of awareness.

And because I had a panty-dropping event with Lariat—whether I'll admit it or not—I'd been struck stupid.

The truck leaps forward as Lariat guns it out of the parking lot and I clutch the cheap vinyl material of the bench seat.

I continue to watch Tommy until my eyes can't see him.

Flopping back down on the seat, I fling my forearm over my eyes. *What a disaster.*

"Who's the prick?"

I close my eyes, a ragged exhale sliding out from between my throbbing lips. I lightly touch the most tender spot on my lower lip and hiss. My fingertip comes away with a single drop of ruby red blood.

"Tommy."

"Why's he beating the shit out of a woman lawyer?"

Lariat's question is excellent, one of many I don't want to answer.

First things first. "I wasn't doing too bad," I defend sullenly.

He snorts, handling the jerking truck with expertise. Lariat shoves the gearshift, and the truck lumbers reluctantly forward.

"You seem like you know what you're doing."

I open my eyes, dropping my arm to the bench seat as I flick my eyes to the rearview mirror to see if he's making fun of me.

Lariat's black gaze is steady on my face. It's hard to hide anything I'm feeling in my discombobulated and disoriented state.

"I was stupid," I admit, dabbing at my lip again and coming up with more blood. *Goddammit.* I have a court trial beginning this week, and I'm all beaten up.

Real professional, Angel.

"I don't think that's how I'd describe you," Lariat says with slow deliberation.

My outfit is in tatters, I look like shit, and have puke breath. Yeah, I'm a real prize.

"I should have been aware of my surroundings once I was outside the safety of the crowd. I know better. He got me because I was all—*gah*." I huff in frustration then grit my teeth against what the movement cost me.

"It was my animal magnetism. Got ya all hot and bothered, and you just stumbled into his trap."

"Please," I say because his assessment is a little too close to the truth for me. But he makes me smile, and I wince as my face moves.

He shrugs, and his muscles bunch as he smoothly shifts again.

"Where are we going?" I'm hoping to change the subject from my embarrassing mess.

"Don't mind tellin ya, but I want to know about this Tommy prick first."

Here goes. "Mob," I say in a curt answer, studiously avoiding his eyes. Instead, I gaze at the torn ceiling upholstery again. I'll have it memorized before long.

"Fuck *me*," he says softly, punching the steering wheel. "That's not good."

Guilt surges through me because I inadvertently involved him. *Not* part of my plan. "Yeah. I'm really sorry. It's my disaster, and you just stepped in without knowing what was really going on." I lightly massage my sternum, trying to self-comfort.

I close my eyes, wanting to cry. I need the money for my client, whom I've already gotten overly involved with. I'm getting in deeper with Lariat by the moment because not only does he hold the purse stings for Mini's freedom, but he saved my ass from Tommy.

I haul myself upright, happy that I'm not seeing everything in triplicate. "Where are we going?"

It's so dark wherever we are, I can only make out shapes.

"Club Prez's cabin. All us guys take a turn living there until we get permanent digs."

"Oh." I don't know Lariat. I've allowed myself to be taken by a stranger. *So dumb.* Maybe not as dumb as being unguarded enough that Tommy was able to beat me, but close.

After we travel what seems like an impossibly long driveway, Lariat directs the truck around a semi-circular drive, puts the gear in park, and kills the engine.

He swings around, his large hand gripping the seat between us. "You okay?"

I nod. "I'll live."

His smile is crooked from disbelief. "Yeah, not the same."

No, it's not. My return smile is genuine. Sarcasm is chased back by gratitude.

He slaps the seat and hops out then opens the back door. I scoot across the long bench, and he grabs my waist. He plucks me out of the back as though I weigh nothing and sets me on my feet.

I look down. I'm missing a heel. *Wonderful.* Sighing, I kick off the other one and gingerly pick it up, tossing it in the back. "What a mess."

Lariat smiles and nods. "Class A snafu."

I laugh, not understanding the acronym. "What?"

"Situation normal, all fucked up."

I giggle, and the laughter rolls into slow sobbing.

Lariat awkwardly pats my shoulder.

I'm so pissed that I'm falling apart, I glare up at him through the wash of tears.

"It's okay if you're like—freaking out or something." He lifts a massive shoulder.

"I'm not freaking out!" I scream, hands fisted by my sides.

"Uh-huh." He folds his arms across his broad chest, his eyes at half-mast. "You can admit you're scared."

I'm so scared about the potential of Tommy that the sweat chills against my skin thinking about it. He'll find me again. And he'll be more determined than ever.

My chin sinks to my chest.

"Hey." Lariat dips low to prop a finger underneath my jaw.

We stare at each other, and his touch against my skin is a branding of flame. His Adam's apple bobs as he swallows hard.

We're hyper aware of each other. There's no denying or hiding it. The vibe is a state of being.

"You're here. You're safe now, Angela."

I cover my face with my hands and stand there like a shaking mess.

Lariat's arms go around me, holding me tight. For just that moment, I allow myself to sink into the comfort another human being is offering me, which is as rare an event as a total eclipse of the sun.

"It's Angel," I whisper.

Lariat leans back, looking down at me with an inscrutable expression.

After a moment more, he nods. "Suits you."

I don't know if the nickname does, but a happy thrill zings through me that he thinks so.

And therein lies the problem.

Happy doesn't happen to me. It's for others.

LARIAT

Damn. Damn. *Damn.*

I'm done for.

I leave Ms. Monroe—Angel—in the makeshift, tightly laid out living area, which is hardly more than a bachelor's pad, and admit that I fucked up.

I stride to the bathroom door, walk through, jerk open the medicine cabinet, and take the blue med kit out by its handle. I pivot, frog marching my ass to the couch where she's sitting.

Elegant legs are crossed at the ankles, and her stockings are run to shit. Her long-fingered, slim hands dangle off the sides of the couch, limp and unanimated.

"Gotta patch you up," I say in a gruff voice.

I probably sound like that because I'm still pissed as fuck. When I came out of Garcia's and caught that prick putting his hands on her, I saw red.

I was instantly back in the sandbox—reactive, instinctive, and deliberate. There was no thought process.

Anger has no place in war, but sometimes the fuel of rage helps the battle.

She gives a slight shake of her head. "I need to—hell—I don't know what I need to do." Angel pushes her hair behind her ear and winces.

That's when I notice half of her hair is in a hair tie, and the rest is all twisted and scattered. Long, silky black strands hang between her tits. And those are pretty much on full display since that mob asshole Tommy tore half her blouse apart.

She seems to notice where my gaze is directed and flicks the shreds of material to cover the lacy black bra.

The bra matches the sexy panties I got a glimpse of before everything went to hell.

"Do you have anything I can put on?"

Hell yes. Me.

My eyes dip to her rack again, and I give another hard swallow. I don't want anything to cover those. "Yeah."

I set the med kit down and make my way to the small bedroom tucked into the back corner of the cabin. I rummage through the battered old chest of drawers and come up with a beat-up Road Kill MC T-shirt—black, like all my other shit.

I walk out with it, and she's unbuttoning her blouse. Her eyes shift to mine. "Do you mind?"

"Nope." I rock back on my heels, boner at full tilt. I'm loving the striptease angle, purposefully misunderstanding the inferred request to turn around and not watch.

Her exhale is irritated. "Listen, I just got my butt kicked, and my clothes are in ruins. I'm not here to be fodder for your teenage boy fantasy."

I move fast, and her eyes widen.

Jerking her up by the arms, I crush her against me. I sink my fingers into her hair, mindful of her injured face.

Her heart beats wildly against my chest, and those big luminescent eyes widen a touch with her fear. "I'm *not* a teenage boy." I press my erection against her stomach. "That feel in any way like a trumped-up hormone blitz?"

Angel shakes her head. "What is this?" she asks in a low voice.

Our bodies are molded together like perfectly fitted pieces of a puzzle.

"I don't know. I'm not much about analyzing shit that feels right." The hand not holding her hair runs down her back, and what's left of her blouse balls in my grasp. I flatten my palm against the small of her back and look into her eyes. "And this feels right." My eyes travel down what I can see of her from the barely there distance. "You do."

I don't usually have to talk so much. Chicks spread em. It's like clockwork. I crook my finger, and they're on their backs. It works.

"The only thing that's right between us is you helped me when I was down. Literally. And you've agreed to aid your cousin."

Her words are cold water, and my hard-on softens. I release her.

Angel's hand moves to her ribs.

I'm a selfish bastard. I take in her face. A bruise like a multi-petaled purple flower is beginning to take shape beneath her eyes and spreading over her cheekbone, a dark bloom of color to match. Angry red morphs to dark grape, starting along her ribcage.

I reach out, running fingers down her side where the shape of a shoe is obvious. "That fucker." My jaw clenches. "I didn't do enough."

Angel sighs, wrapping her smaller hand around mine that's against her rib.

I'm not dumb enough to mistake her action for more. Angel has made it clear that my dick's not going in her.

"You've done too much." Her eyes touch mine then jerk away. "Now he'll let the family know who you are, and they'll hurt you too."

She lets my hand go and shifts away from me.

"Fuck them. I'm Road Kill MC. The mob doesn't fuck with us; we don't fuck with them."

Angel shakes her head. "You don't get it."

I get way more than she knows.

"Tommy is just a lackey. They'll send him again, or someone else to intimidate me."

44

I cross my arms, looking over the various damage this prick inflicted on her body.

Makes me want to kick his ass again.

"Why is the mob bothering you? You're a high-profile woman. It doesn't make a lot of sense."

Angel nods, raising an eyebrow. "Since you won't be a gentleman and turn around while I change."

I snort.

She jerks off her blouse and stands in front of me. The inky shade of the fabric on her body boldly contrasts with skin like a porcelain doll's. Turning, she tosses the tattered blouse on the armrest of the couch, with a frown. She tears my T-shirt over her head, spreading more of her black hair around her and covering the great view of her tits—as well as the bruise that dick put on her.

"I had a man I was defending." She twists her hands together, and I have a sudden surge of tenderness. I viciously clamp down the alien emotion.

"His was the only testimony against the local mob boss. We had him in witness protection—the entire thing. He couldn't afford some of the high-profile attorneys, and I was hungry, fresh out of law school. Going to take on the world. Save it. Get on the map." She gives a small shake of her head as though chastising the person she used to be, and her eyes meet mine. Raw pain washes through them before she looks away.

I wonder about that elusive emotion but shelve the expression on her face to think about later.

"Anyway"—she tosses a chunk of hair behind her shoulder—"they got him."

"So the boss got away with it?"

Angel shakes her head, and her eyes rise to meet mine again. "No." Her voice is a whisper. "We nailed Ricci, but then he found my client later. His family did, and they made an example of him."

I could take a guess at the example they used, but Angel fills in the blanks without me having to ask.

"They hung him by his intestines." She shudders.

I don't react with revulsion. *Seen worse.* But I say nothing for a few seconds. "How do you come into it?"

Angel talks to her hands. "I speculate the mob boss still blames me. He's doing time because, essentially, I spearheaded his jail stint. Now there's some mob loser who comes knocking every so often. Probably everyone who was involved with putting the boss away will suffer."

I feel my brows knot together. "Tell the cops. Hot lawyer chick like yourself. Act helpless." I lift my chin, leveling my gaze at her. "Should be easy to pull off."

She snorts. "Lot of them are on the payroll. Don't know which is what." Angel lifts a shoulder.

I wag a finger at her. "We get you into the station, show them the damage. Hell, I was there. I witnessed it."

Her eyes spear mine just as fiercely. "And you kicked his ass then took off. You'll get in trouble too."

She's right. Keep forgetting she knows the law. I scrape a palm over my head. Fuck. I'm going to have to go to church on this one.

I slide my cell out of the interior pocket of my cut and text Viper. The prez of Road Kill MC will decide what action there is to be taken, if any. I already stepped in a pile of steaming shit by kicking somebody's ass who is with the mob. In my own defense, it wasn't as though he was wearing a sign.

Personally, I'm a wait-and-see type of man. But many heads are better than just my thick skull on this cluster-fuck. I finish tapping out my message, grin crookedly over how pissed Vipe will be to get this particular text, and slide my cell back in my pocket. Viper is *not* tech-savvy. That's a no-shitter.

"Who'd you contact?"

"Road Kill Prez."

Her delicate eyebrows knit together. "I don't want this becoming a biker gang matter."

I narrow my gaze at her. "We're not a gang. Don't disrespect the club, Angel, because you're disrespecting me." I thumb my chest.

"I'm sorry," she says quietly. "I meant it when I said thank you. And I'll admit I don't have a vast wealth of knowledge regarding motorcycle clubs. But your club getting more involved just means I have more people I'm responsible for. And I don't want to be responsible for someone else getting killed."

I walk to her and sink to my haunches. "Wait a fucking second, Angel." I grab her hand, and it lies in my hold like a limp noodle. I cradle her chilled fingers and take a stab at communicating. Talking is not my best strength. "You're not responsible for some dude getting offed because the mob took it into their heads that they wanted a slice of revenge."

I lift her chin again with a bent knuckle. It seems I'm doing a lot of that shit tonight. "They can't continue to threaten you." I search her eyes, trying to force her to get the message. "That's a fucked-up way to live. Constantly under fear of getting beat up." *Raped,* I think but don't say.

She shakes her head free of my grip. "Don't help me."

I abruptly change the subject. "Where'd you learn how to defend yourself?"

Angel's quiet so long that I don't think she'll answer. "When I was young, I needed to have those skills. If Tommy hadn't taken me by surprise, I would have handed him his balls."

I chuckle, flashing a fierce grin. "I believe it."

Her smile is just as spontaneous. "You're an okay guy when you're not being crude every second."

I shrug. *Truth time.* "I'm honest. If that makes me crude, so be it." I hate the feeling of not being on her level. She's top-shelf, and I'm a rough guy from a poor background. I'm solid, though. Anyone who knows me would vouch for me.

But Angela Monroe doesn't know me. Come to think of it, she doesn't really matter. I'm getting my boxers in a twist over a chick. Hell, sweet butts are plentiful. I don't need this angsty shit.

Emotional entanglements are for guys intent on sprouting uteruses.

Her lips twist in sad irony. "Yeah, you're honest, all right."

I'm getting pissed off again. "Listen, you take the bed, and I'll sleep on the couch." I stand before I open my trap and say shit I can't take back.

She stands too, wincing, and my eyes go to the hand on her side. "Thank you, but I'm not spending the night here."

I feel my brows hop.

Her eyes roam my face. "I'm sorry. I mean—I'm grateful. But I want to go home, take a shower, fix myself up, brush my teeth." She grimaces, and I remind myself she got knocked around pretty good. I haven't done anything to clean her up. The med box sits between us, untouched.

I plant my hands on my hips. "Probably need to have a doctor check you out."

Angel vigorously shakes her head, which causes her to sway.

I grab her elbow, and our gazes lock.

Her arm tenses inside my hold, but she doesn't try to break free.

"Will you take me home?"

I shake my head. "No way, won't get a wink of shut-eye. I'll be thinking about some dickhead—Tommy or some other chump—coming by and doing a repeat performance."

Angela Monroe's just another chick. Uh-huh.

Angel sighs and looks around for a few seconds at the sparse surroundings of the cabin, which is kind of an abbreviated bachelor's pad. "Fine. I guess there's some logic there."

I roll my eyes to the ceiling. *Yeah. Hallelujah.*

My attention moves back to her. "Use the head. Take a shower. Spare toothbrush's under the sink. Knock yourself out."

She rolls her bottom lip between her teeth, clearly indecisive.

"Not gonna attack ya. I'm not fucking desperate." Shit, that sounded bad, as if she's fugly or something.

Angela's jaw pulls back, and her eyes skate away. "I see. Okay, well, I'll do that then."

"I didn't mean I had to be desperate to think you're…" *Fuck.* I don't say anything more, figuring I can come out ahead if I shut my running mouth.

She turns away from me and walks slowly to the bathroom door then softly shuts it behind her.

That went bad as fuck.

My cell vibrates with a call. I take it out and look at the incoming name.

I swipe.

"Hey."

"Vipe says there's an emergency church in the morning." The question in Noose's voice bleeds through the cell.

I guess there is, but Viper hasn't gotten back to me. Of course, he would never text.

Noose gets right to the point. He and I haven't settled everything between us from when we served together. Saying our relationship is strained is an understatement. I think he mishandled some shit. He thinks I'm harboring resentment I shouldn't be.

We're both probably right. But sometimes, a disagreement begins and takes on a life of its own. It's as though we can't remember why we're so pissed at each other. But the shit sits there, festering like a wound that won't heal.

"Rose is making pancakes. I hate leaving the house for avoidable bullshit. Better be motherfucking good."

Fine. "Listen, don't be a dick. Got a lawyer chick I had to meet about my cousin."

"The one you haven't seen in ten years?" His voice is filled with sarcasm.

I clench my jaw. "Yeah, that one."

Noose lets the silence beat between us for almost half a minute. Finally he says, "Gotta be fucking dumb for a lawyer to be involved."

"Hundred grand bail worth of dumb."

Noose whistles low. "Fuck me. That blows."

I grunt. "Yeah. Bail's set."

"What'd she do?"

"Killed her old man."

Noose doesn't say anything for a beat. "She a psycho bitch type?"

The translation is *Great in the sack but crazy.*

It's not like I would fucking know. Christ. "Nah. He was using his fists on her pretty regularly."

"Okay, so Miss Lawyer is at Vipe's cabin?" He doesn't rein in the sarcasm. "That was fast."

"Not like that. Not banging her. Saved her."

"Okay, stop speaking in riddles. Out with it."

"Some fuck started beating her up the minute she got out of the bar."

"*What?*" Noose is clearly puzzled.

"Yeah, mob putz."

"That's worth church," Noose admits slowly.

I can't argue his assessment because it was the same as mine. "Yup."

"You keeping her safe for now?"

Is it that transparent? "Yeah."

"Getting a case of the feels, Lariat?"

I squeeze the cell's housing, and it groans under my abuse. "Fuck. Off."

Noose barks out a laugh. "Not gonna lie. I'm *so* liking this."

"Don't like anything too much, you big prick."

Silence fills the line for a moment.

"See ya at church, Lancelot."

Ass. I swipe his smug face from my phone and set it on the scarred end table beside the couch.

I strip my socks and boots off, chuck my shit along the base of the couch, and lie there, staring at the tongue-and-groove-planked ceiling.

Listening to the soft patter of water, I think about Angel lathering her body up.

I adjust my junk, pissed that she's forced me to give shits about all this.

And that I've allowed it to matter.

5

ANGEL

I spread the slick folds of my labia, desperate for relief.

A person might say I'm insane, that sexual arousal is not possible after getting beaten up while in the company of some bike gang member.

But I would say that pain, fear, and chemistry can be inexplicably mixed like a perfect cocktail.

And damned if Lariat hasn't worked me up into a lather that's from more than the soap I hold in my hands.

I clean and rub, my fingertip grazing softly along my clit as I twirl it.

Panting, I hang my head. The hot water from the shower cascades down my back and runs between the split of my ass cheeks.

"Close," I whisper to myself.

Just as my pussy comes to full attention and I'm on the brink of an orgasm, a hard pounding sounds at the bathroom door.

Squeezing my thighs together, I restrain myself from giving a frustrated scream. Then I realize what that would provoke: Lariat charging through the door, finding me wet, naked, and suffering from blue clit.

Just what I don't need.

"What?" I croak then clear my throat. "What is it?"

"You okay in there? Ya drowning? It's been a half hour."

I'm squeaky clean, and I was going to blow a proper cork of sexual tension you've so miserably given me. *Thank you very much.*

"Just trying to get the filth off," I say out loud.

No comment.

But I can feel his presence outside the door. I imagine the fingertips of those large hands spread against the other side of the wood. Of course, that leads me to envision them inside of me, and I bite back a small moan.

Only the water smacking the porcelain shower basin sounds between us.

I swear I can hear his breathing, and when he does speak, I jump.

"Want me in there?"

Holy shit. No.

Yes.

A handful of seconds float between us.

"I'm not beggin ," he says.

God, me either.

We're wrong on about a hundred different levels, but I know when I want that itch scratched. I don't need any complications with a man. Relationships are for whole people—people who want commitment.

But this man doesn't. I can tell. He's a safe fuck.

I shut the water off and move to the door, naked and wet. Stupid. *Brave.*

Horny.

I fling the door open.

Lariat's black eyes widen a smidgen.

I smile.

He doesn't. Instead, his eyes feast on my body, and I'm glad I run, do squats, and am slightly obsessive with exercise.

It's what I *can* control in my life.

"I'm not gonna last with you, Angel." His voice is strained, and I feel powerful that I've moved this hard man.

"Let's see."

I walk toward him, my earlier reserve lost to the moment, the volatility of the night, our meeting, and the combustible tether cinching us.

I press my naked breasts against his chest and dampen his clothes. He sucks in a breath so sharp, it sounds painful.

Lariat's arms wrap me tightly against him and lift me up as he crushes his mouth to mine.

We don't talk. I wrap my nakedness around him, legs twisting around his torso and arms encircling his thick neck.

He groans, and I press my most tender part against his flat, tight stomach.

"Clothes," he rasps.

I break our brutal kiss long enough to command, "Lose them."

"Bossy bitch." But his smile is soft.

I bite his lip, just shy of drawing blood, and the look he gives makes me shiver.

Hot.

Chilled.

Lariat spins us and walks to a bedroom I noticed earlier that was only a dark hole with a door.

Extracting my arms and legs, he tosses me in the air. I can't see anything, and my hands reactively fly out to stop my contact.

A soft bed catches me, and I bounce once.

My eyes travel his huge body, which is silhouetted by the vague amber glow of ancient nightlights.

The leather, patched vest hangs over the doorknob, while he dumps the shirt and jeans unceremoniously on the floor.

His cock is fully erect, unburdened by underwear. The sight catches my breath in my throat.

Naked under his jeans. Ready for anything.

Ready for me.

Lariat's hands fist, and he takes two strides closer. I take in the knuckles that are slightly abraded from him beating a man to save me.

I lie back with a prayer of a sigh and spread my legs for him.

Lariat stares down at my naked body then his fists punch down at either side of my thighs. When he bends over between my thighs, his face hovers, and the look he gives me is pure heat and fire for a single moment before his mouth lands on me.

I thread my fingers through his hair and yank him against my pussy as I lift my hips.

"Eager as fuck," he says in a low growl against my opening. I moan, jerking my hips as high as they can go.

He slides a palm under my ass, and when his finger plunges inside my already soaked channel, his deft tongue finds my clit. I burst apart, coming in a great pulsing wave of pleasure.

"Ah!" I scream, but Lariat doesn't stop or let up.

My throbbing, wet pussy convulses around his pumping finger. His tongue presses against my clit, and the hand that is holding my butt cheeks moves perilously closer to the bud of my ass.

I try to say no—*stop*—it's too much. But I feel another beauty of an orgasm building, so I'm robbed of speech. Instead, I lie there with a man I don't know filling the cavities of my body with flesh and pleasure.

When his thumb dips into my back opening, and his other finger sinks deep, he gives a single hard flick over my clit with his tongue.

I crest again, exploding into a thousand pieces of acute pleasure that's almost pain. My fingertips go numb, and light dances in the periphery of my vision.

Lariat's face is suddenly in front of mine.

I smell myself on him.

He presses his lips to my mouth and kisses me so deeply, we're like one body of movement together.

His erection seats between my legs, slipping on the wetness he made.

"Say yes. Tell me to fuck you," he breathes.

I wrap my legs around his hips, and with thought born only of emotion, I reply, "Fuck me, Lariat."

He throws his head back and plunges his length inside. When he's halfway in, I realize I didn't get a really good look at him.

He's *huge*.

"You're so fucking tight," he groans, burying his face in the crook of my neck.

My happy female bits give a single squeeze, and he shoves himself a little further inside of me, stretching and pressing.

I writhe, trying to catch more of him, deeper—faster.

"Stop! Fuck, Angel, I can't last. You fit me like a glove."

"So good," I whisper and hike my hips just as he rocks forward. His cock finally comes to the end of me, seated as deeply as a man and woman can be.

We throb together, and he rises above me in a classic push-up position. Lariat's eyes search my face, then he does something unexpected—he takes a single strand of hair that is crossed over the bridge of my nose and smooths it away, slowing the moment.

Then he kisses each eyebrow.

My lids flutter shut.

The softest press of lips falls against each lid, and I sigh.

His cock leaves me, and my eyes fly open at its sudden absence. Lariat smiles, sheathing himself again in a thick, sliding press.

I tip my head back, and my eyes roll upward.

His hands cup my ass, lifting me, and he pumps deeply.

"Oh God, yes—fuck me."

I open my eyes and look into the darkness of his gaze. Lariat's stomach muscles bunch and clench as he rides my body on his knees, gripping my hips and plunging in.

When his rhythm speeds, I seamlessly rise to meet him, our eyes locked.

"Gonna come," he says in a hoarse whisper.

I squeeze my legs around his hips and shout my orgasm into the room. My only thought is of his delicious seed spreading deep.

The cords of his neck stand out as he throws his head back. I can't help but notice his beauty as a male.

Our beauty together.

The vision causes joy and anguish.

I come down from my multiple orgasms in floating pieces of ecstasy, like feathers that never land.

Lariat lays his body on top of mine like a blanket of protection.

We fit. I give a delighted shiver, and he presses me closer.

I don't allow myself intimacy, but I allow myself this moment.

And it's enough.

Lariat runs his calloused hand from the tip of my shoulder to the valley of my waist then to the swell of my hip. He wraps his fingers around the rise and bone.

Then he continues the journey over and over.

I tremble from his touch.

Though he's a raw guy, he's apparently too good of a man to point out that I said I wouldn't sleep with him and did anyway.

Yeah. Smooth, Angel.

My silence is complete, and we lie together comfortably, not like the one-night stand we are but scarily as much more.

I can't let assumptions play out. I have to come clean. I doubt Lariat wants more, but I have to bury any potential.

"I—"

His hand folds over my mouth, while his free hand cups my sex.

I suck in a breath and smell him—the sex we had and the subtle smell of soap on his skin. "Don't talk. Don't ruin this."

I close my eyes as his fingers find my moist center, wet with my arousal and wet with his cum.

I kiss the hand against my mouth, and his fingers drop away.

"I have to be honest here, Lariat."

He chuckles. "Feelin like we've been plenty honest."

Heat climbs my face, and I'm intensely glad he can't see my blush.

I feel on fire…alive. For so many different reasons.

Lariat falls away from me. His slick fingers trail over my side, and my chest tightens with the urge to cry. I don't know why I'm getting so emotional.

Oh yeah, it might have to do with my stressful occupation and the fear of reprisal I live under constantly.

"I love having sex with you," I say.

"But," he drawls, knotting his fingers underneath his head.

I hear the biting sarcasm in that one word, hating that it's there, hating that I put it there.

"I'm not into relationships."

"Perfect. Me either." He answers instantly. "We can just fuck."

Here's the hard part. "I don't keep fucking," I admit slowly.

Lariat rolls over, and he's half on me before I take my next breath. His leg pins me to the bed.

I grip his hard biceps. God, he's hot.

Menace is not part of his hold on me, only the promise of more of him inside more of me.

The potential drenches my pussy. I'm already sore from his size and his enthusiasm, which I loved.

But if he said the word, I would go again. Sex doesn't count as two times if it's twice in one night. That's what I tell myself, at least.

Lariat grasps my face with both hands, holding me still. "We are not stopping at one night. Do you know how fucking rare it is to have two people who can make each other feel that way?"

His black eyes are intense, and his words are frighteningly accurate.

I nod at his truth. "Doesn't matter. I can't."

"Can't or won't?"

I squeeze my eyes shut. "Both," I whisper.

Lariat moves away from my body, and I'm cold without him.

After several minutes pass, he says, "Get some shut eye. I'll get ya home in the morning."

His weight leaves the bed, and he pads naked from the bedroom, softly closing the door behind him.

I stare at the solid barrier of wood for a long time.

Sleep finally comes, but it's not restful.

6

LARIAT

God *damn.*

I charge out the front door, naked and not giving one fuck...any fucks.

I want a smoke so bad that I can taste the acrid flavor on my tongue. I gave cancer sticks up when I separated from the navy. I'm not going to start up now.

Cuz of a bitch.

Yeah.

You're a dumb sonaofabitch, Lariat.

I pace the expansive front porch of my borrowed accommodations, loving the solitude.

Or I *did* love the solitude before I decided to be all white knight and shit and save Miss Prissy.

I peg my hands on my hips, and my fingers shake some. Angel has me worked up.

I've never been with a woman that turned me inside out like she does. Angel took charge, and I let her.

She felt right in my hands, soft but lithe, pliable, meant to be held by me. Usually, I don't like tall chicks, but she fits me.

I chuckle. And that pussy strangles my cock in the best way possible.

I shake my head, plunking my ass down on whatever surface will have me. I'll probably get splinters in my ass, but I don't care. I swipe a hand through my short hair and plant my face in my hands.

How did things get this fucked up? How does a chick call the shots in a matter of hours?

She says she won't sleep with me then does. Best fuck of the century. Better than that, even. I *felt* something. It snuck up on me—feeling.

A ton of time has passed since I felt anything but numb. I've been too busy trying to forget the bad shit I did, that we all did.

My mind tries to travel that familiar pathway to the night when Noose and I got intel.

That intel had me killing kids. Kids with guns, but still kids.

The goat farmer we'd been ordered to wax had been Al-Qaeda.

Noose had knotted his ass, deservedly.

My hands quake with the memories. I press my fist to my cheek, biting the inside in an old nervous habit. It's a gesture I thought I'd lost.

I'm too fucking soft. That's my problem. Noose and I have never seen eye to eye on the fucking issue.

His words haunt me in the dark on Viper's porch.

"Fuck them." He'd glared at me, and I know it hadn't been in anger, just sheer frustration over the horrible circumstances. "Those kids would've been Al-Qaeda the instant they could run. They had no choice. They never had a choice."

His light gray eyes had narrowed on me. "Just like you had no choice."

Their small bodies had jumped and danced in the pale silver moonlight, illuminating their deaths forever.

That dance continues to replay, burnt into my memory.

The men I served with tell me the women they committed to help them live without the constant ghost of violence hanging in their heads like a noxious vapor. Noose, Wring, even Snare, have all fallen to the almighty pussy whip.

I'm the only holdout.

I don't know if I can believe them, that there would be any reprieve from my fucked-up thoughts. But for an hour or two tonight, I wasn't in my head.

That time had been spent with Angela Monroe.

I chuckle. *Can't fuck her twenty-four hours a day to forget.* But the potential to have some kind of existence free of the lingering foulness of my deeds is a sweet motivator.

However, Angel says she *just* fucks. One time.

Makes me think she's as slutty as any sweet butt that shoves her snatch and tits in our faces at the club.

What makes Angel any better?

Everything. That single revelation weaves sorrowfully through my mind.

I'm so fucked.

But I'm not begging. That'll be the day when I have to convince a bitch that she needs to be with me.

Standing, I stretch, lightly tapping the solid wood porch ceiling with my fingertips.

Dawn spreads icy fingers of white light over the forest and hills that surround the lone cabin. The woodland appears to breathe awake with a pale light frosted by gold.

My eyes hunt the hills, remembering another country with mounds of sand and heat. The land was so dry, thinking of one's own saliva could make a man thirsty.

I shake the cloying memory off as a board creeks behind me.

I whirl, crouching as my arms swing in a semicircle.

It's Angel, looking like her namesake. She stands there, wearing only my black Road Kill MC T-shirt.

Her nipples pebble against the dark fabric in the chill of early morning.

Just like that, I want to fuck her again.

My dick betrays me, sticking out like a divining rod toward water.

Angel doesn't look down but at my face, searching the residual expressions left behind from my thoughts. "What is it?"

Fuck. I hold back a shudder. *She sees me.* I can't have that. I shut down my expression, thinking of a few choice torture events.

Losing the boner, I gain my frozen exterior back.

"Nothing, why?" I bark, more harshly than I mean to.

Angel shrugs warily, appearing to sense my mood. "I don't know." She looks away, her eyes traveling the same scene mine just went over. "You seemed a little lost is all."

Angel has to go before she unravels secrets I don't even know I have.

I swing a hard smirk. "I'm naked, not lost."

Her eyes swing back and roam my body. When she's through with her slow perusal, her chartreuse eyes lock with mine. "You're beautiful, Lariat. Truly."

I grunt. I hate the compliment, but I crave it. Which makes me hate it all over again.

I ignore her words, shouldering past her into the cabin. I gather my jeans from the couch where I dumped them and stalk into the room where we just fucked.

My eyes flick to the door.

The bed is made as though we were never in it. My cut is laid out on top.

"You made the bed." My voice is utterly empty. Is she trying to erase our time together?

I pivot, facing her, prepared to be angry, and she's right there, close enough to touch.

Angel nods. "Yes."

My hands ball into fists. "You ashamed of being with me?"

She frowns as if the question is stupid. "Never."

My hands unclench, and my shoulders drop. Maybe I've gauged shit wrong. That would be rare. I'm pretty fucking good at understanding undertones. I've needed to be.

Her hand rises, and I snatch it before she can touch me. What I really want to do is kiss its center until she melts against me.

"I'll take ya home now."

My eyes move to our hands, my hold on hers. Her hand is so small in mine. I release her.

Angel gives me a sad little smile that makes me wonder. But her words were clear. I don't remember everything she said word for word. But the gist of it is that she fucks. Once. Then she boots the guy to the curb.

And Lariat is not going to be yesterday's trash.

She nods, looks down at her bare legs, and walks back into the bedroom. When she comes out a couple of minutes later, her skirt is back in place and her wrecked blouse is in her hand.

Angel lifts her blouse. "Guess this is kaput."

My smile is genuine. "Yeah." I kind of feel as though fate brought us together, at least for the night. I *really* want to regret her.

But I can't.

Best sex I ever had. Or maybe it was the best connection.

I'm not going to analyze the difference.

☠

We pull up to Garcia's Bar and Grill in the bright light of Sunday morning. Everything looks whitewashed, glaring back at us. The magic of the bar and how we met is overshadowed by what Tommy did. Angel's side will hold bruises for a couple of weeks. Her face has a shiner just offset from her left eye.

I scan the parking lot a second time. Tommy's gone like I knew the sack of shit would be.

Her car's not. My eyes widen. Too bad it's completely fucked.

Angel seems shell-shocked, taking in the tiny tin can she calls a car. Her fingertips bite into the seat on either side of where she sits.

I throw the truck into park and hop out. My eyes seek the corners of the parking lot a third time, assessing.

I stride to the passenger door and open it.

Angel looks down at me, her eyes shining with tears. *Tough girl.* If she loved her car, I wouldn't know it.

"You okay?" My voice is gruff. I don't want her to get the wrong impression—that I give a shit. It's still a tough break, though. She got her ass kicked, and her ride is fucked.

She gives a single nod, and a stubborn, fat tear slides down her cheek. Just one.

Scrubbed free of makeup, her face is even more beautiful—not classically, like some made-up model, but real beauty.

She slides out of the truck and walks, uncaring of her bare feet, to the driver's side.

A hole about the size of a fist is plugged through the driver's side window. The size looks like it would fit the end of a bat to me.

Angel's laugh sounds like brittle glass falling.

I wince at the sound.

"Fuck," she says softly. The curse word sounds wrong coming from her mouth in this context. It didn't so much when we were sexing it up at the cabin.

My gaze travels the length of the car. There's no driving this vehicle anywhere. All four tires are slashed, and the window is the least of the abuse.

"This is just perfect." Angel swipes angrily at another tear. "I'm beat up, my car's unusable, and I have court this week."

"Hello," I say from the peanut gallery, lifting an arm in the air like a student waiting for the teacher to notice him.

Angel whirls, and I throw up my other arm to join the first. "Thinking work might not matter when you're considering the alternative." I slap my arms against my sides.

Angel puts her hands on her hips. She looks hot when she's in a rage.

I smirk.

She stomps over to where I stand and pokes me in the chest.

"Don't be poking me, Angel." My voice is low and dangerous.

Her eyes flash like flames. "Don't laugh at my situation."

"Not laughing." I capture her finger and suck it into my mouth.

Her lips part.

I move it back and forth, fucking her finger like I did her sweet pussy just hours ago.

The pupils in Angel's golden-green eyes dilate.

"Thinking you should be taking things slow"—*smack, suck, lick*—"instead of flying around like a target."

I release her finger, and her hand drops limply by her side. She blinks up at me then covers her face as though she's hiding. "I can't do this anymore. I want to be decent, be the good guy."

"Girl," I correct automatically.

She nods, wiping her nose, which is now red with snot and tears.

"But these idiots keep trying to intimidate me. They're never going to succeed."

"They will if you're dead," I say quietly.

Her gaze meets mine. "Do you think they would really kill me? While their dumb godfather cools his heels in jail?"

Fear takes up residency in my gut. "Yup."

She crosses her arms, leaning away from me.

Here we go.

"And what do you know about mob stuff, Big Bad Biker?"

Gripping her upper arms, I haul her toward me. "I know bad when I see it and could smell that numb nuts Tommy a mile away. They won't quit until you do something to get him out. They killed the only witness. They're putting the squeeze on you so you'll recant or do whatever lawyer shit you can do."

"There's no recanting, Lariat. It's the *witness's* testimony, and he's gone."

Dead.

I shake my head, dismissing the obvious shit. The shit somebody can see. "Then they have another angle. Maybe they'll manipulate you onto their side."

Her beautiful eyes narrow, and I instantly want her again. Right here. Right now.

Not just for a night.

I swallow against the raw emotion and stuff that shit deep inside. "Lay low. Don't make a bull's-eye outta yourself. Fuck court."

Angel wrenches her arms away from me. "Forget court, huh?" She shakes her head in clear disbelief. "There's no *forgetting* court."

"Is your life worth it?"

She can't take back the pause or the shadow that slides through her eyes.

"Is it?" I yell.

She startles and looks down. "No," she whispers.

"Glad we figured that shit out."

I walk back to her, grab her hand, and begin towing her back to the truck.

"What?" she sputters.

I jerk my chin toward the cab. "Hop in. I'll get ya home."

She resists.

I turn, giving a chuckle of disbelief. "Listen, you're not driving that mauled tin can. Ya can't, even if you want to."

We look at the trashed compact car.

"It's a smart car," she mutters.

I chuckle. "Uh-huh. Lookin pretty dumb from where I stand."

Angel doesn't say anything; she just gets in and slams the door.

7

ANGEL

I hug my body and think about my day, car and my face—all ruined.

Well, except for the horizontal workout I did with Lariat. That part was salvageable..

I slide a glance his way.

Strong hands grip the wheel of the beat-up truck we're riding in as he smoothly maneuvers through Meridian Valley Country Club. Hands wield the truck expertly, hands that were tender and thorough on my body just hours ago.

I release the hold on my body and point to a cream-colored, low-slung, 1950s ranch-style house. "That's it."

Lariat doesn't say anything as he tightly parks the car along the curb.

"You could've parked in the drive." It's not as though I have a car to park there.

Tears tighten my throat for the second time today, and I twist my fingers together, trying like hell to keep the wetness at bay.

"Truck leaks oil like a sieve. Don't want to dirty up your pretty driveway."

I swing my face to his, my eyes narrowing to slits.

A vague smile hangs on his full lips. There's something about the *things* he says. They sound as though he has a chip on his shoulder, and I'm the cause.

Lariat sure didn't have a chip last night when he fucked me. I was just *fine* then.

I turn my body toward his, ready for a fight, or just *ready*. Gooseflesh creeps over my body, a solid precursor to rage. "What exactly *is* your problem?" I bite out.

His black eyebrows hike. "Problem?" He has the nerve to look vaguely puzzled.

"Yes. You want to fight? You don't like where I live or what I represent to you? Fine. We fucked it out last night. So you like me enough for *that*."

Fresh ruddy color creeps up his strong neck. And I know I'm poking the snake.

I don't care at all.

Springing up on my knees, I get in his face, my voice vibrating with stress, hurt, and fear. My ribs protest my moving, forgetting they're hurt, and I ignore the pain.

"Just because you have issues, doesn't mean you need to shit all over me!"

I sit back down, swivel, and pop the door latch. I drop out of the cab of the truck. Then I notice I have bare feet, and it's October. I wince. Whatever.

I hike my purse from the floorboard and stomp to my front door without bothering to shut the passenger side of the truck. I just want to be away from Lariat and his condemnation.

The keys in my hand jingle noisily as I turn them in the lock and shove the door open.

Jerk!

I go to slam the door closed, but Lariat's palm slaps it open. The solid wood bangs against the wall, and I back away from him. The keys are still plugged into the lock and jangle from the violent motion.

His face is contained thunder. "Don't walk away from me, Angel."

"Pfft!" I whistle through my teeth. "You don't own me. It was *one* night. And I'm grateful that you charged in and stopped Tommy from hurting me further. But you and I"—I whip a finger between us—"we don't work. You're pissed about who I am and can't get past it long enough to stop slinging shit at me like a hyper monkey. Loved what you do for me in the sack, but it's not enough. Let's just call it good." I clench my jaw.

Lariat strides forward without a word and grabs me.

I gasp, dumping my purse on the floor. My lipstick, tampons, and other stuff roll out.

Lariat's fingers sink into my hair, and he tips my head back with a near-painful hold. He searches my eyes, and his gaze travels to my mouth a heartbeat before his lips crash against mine.

I groan inside his mouth. Our tongues twine and lash in a near-frenzy.

He sweeps me up, and my legs go automatically around his torso.

Lariat sucks his lips off mine. His eyes flick to the door and notice it's open. He turns, kicking it shut.

"What—" I try before he whips his head back and his lips latch onto my mouth again.

Coming up for air, he grates, "Bedroom."

I shake my head, and he drives me against the wall instead. The only thing saving me from being hurt is one of his large hands bracing me before impact, while the other cups my ass.

My skirt is hiked once again, panties long gone. His upper body pins me as his hand dives between us. Then his jeans drop to his ankles.

Sans underwear, his cock finds my wet opening and dives in with a single thrust.

We scream together, and I lock my thighs tighter around his hips, arms clinging to his neck.

His thrusting is powerful, and my back slides against the wall. Something glass falls beside us, and Lariat buries his face in the crook of my neck. "Love how you feel," he rumbles.

I go even wetter, if possible, my arousal starting to moisten my inner thighs around his pumping cock.

I widen around his pounding, and he digs deeper, spearing my center, holding nothing back. This isn't tender. It's intense, frantic.

Just what I need.

The orgasm takes me by surprise, sneaking up and attacking me.

I pulse around Lariat's huge cock in great sucking waves. He cries out as if he's in pain, escaping my body and slamming his thickness back in with a final deep rock, sheathing himself tightly inside of me and spurting his seed deep.

I lean against his shoulder, panting, spent, exhausted.

I broke my own rule. Twice now. *What have I done?*

I roll my head to the side, feeling his thumping heartbeat. His skin warms mine as he pins me against the wall.

Lariat slowly pulls his face away, and we look at each other, still connected, though he's softening inside me. "Don't know what the fuck just happened," he admits in a vaguely dazed voice.

We just had sex. *Again.* That's what happened.

He flat palms my sweaty hair out of my face. His voice goes low. "Did I hurt you?"

I shake my head but can't speak. I clear my throat and try again. "No."

We stare at each other. He smiles first, and then we're grinning. "You are incredible, Angel."

He deserves truth. "You're not so bad yourself."

"Not bad, huh?" His eyes hood, and Lariat leans close, doing something with his hips. My pussy gives a single, happy pulse as he slips out.

"Maybe amazing," I reluctantly admit, my voice breathy.

He smirks, but it's not one of those flinty types he shoots around like marbles. It's soft, thoughtful, as his eyes hover over my face.

Carefully, he sets me on my feet and lowers to his knees. The position puts him directly in front of my vagina.

I blink.

He tugs and carefully rolls my skirt down, smoothing the tight material over my hips. He lays his head against the fabric, his cheek over the top of my pubic bone. Wrapping his arms around my ass, he hikes me, and I fall over his shoulder.

"What!" I shout against his back, but laughter is in there too.

"Gonna clean you up," he announces. Something inside me eases, hearing him sounding soft—lighter.

Lariat finds the bathroom and drags me down the front of him. He's so much taller that I have to crane my neck to look at him—a first. With his boots on, he is nearly six feet six, I would say. He's a monster of a man.

He's a man I think I'm taming. Because make no mistake—Lariat is wild, caged.

I see it in his eyes. Some of what he's lived and done slides through eyes so dark I can't make out the pupil, even in the bright light cast by the bathroom fixture.

He reaches over and uses a type of braille to turn on the faucet for the shower, never taking those ebony eyes off mine.

I hear the water come on, and the drops make a hissing sound as they come into contact with the tumbled travertine basin.

I raise my arms above my head, and he takes my shirt off. Expert fingers remove my bra, and his head dips low. He takes first one nipple into his mouth then moves on to the other, laving and sucking with his tongue.

My pussy tingles, and even as sore as I am, I want him inside me again.

I thread my hands through his short hair but have nothing to hold on to. My eyelids slide open, and he's gazing at me as though he wants to memorize my face.

"Get in," he says, indicating the shower with a hike of his chin.

I unzip my skirt and let the fabric pool at my feet in a circle of black. I step out of the middle and into the shower. Water hits every mark made by Tommy, and I suck in a sharp breath.

Lariat's hand is there in an instant, easing down my side. He tickles me, and my lips curl into a smile as I laugh.

"Tickles," I say.

His face is so solemn, it steals my laughter as he takes his hand back through the opening of my shower.

The glass block obscures him for a moment then reveals him before me again. He's so broad that he moves through the opening of the shower sideways then faces me dead-on. Though he's dark-complexioned, he does not have a lot of body hair. He has more than a five o'clock shadow peppering his square jaw, offsetting the inky short hair on his head.

We stare at each other, and he blinks, chasing the water away from his eyes with a hard flick of his head. "Come ere."

I walk to him, and our fingers lace. He turns my wrists under and pulls me against him. I lay my face between the strong planes of his chest.

With agonizing slowness, he unwinds the fingers of our hands and runs his palm down my spine.

I shiver, and he holds me tighter as he backs me up into the water.

We don't speak as he lathers his hands with a bar of soap he grabs off the shelf. Lariat carefully runs his hands over every part of me, even the injuries. I can't help but make little noises of pain as even his lightest touch still hurts those tender areas.

Lariat's eyes skate to mine, darkening with anger.

"I could kick his ass again."

I believe him, because the look in his eyes is crystal clear.

"Actually"—his hand palms my waist—"I could do more."

Murder.

His eyes meet mine, and I witness that lethal potential but don't comment.

Lariat misses none of my body, his hands sliding tenderly over my female parts. I kick one foot up on his shoulder as he kneels before me and washes the bottoms of my feet.

I lean back against the tile, palms flat on either side of my body. As his mouth finds my center, I cry out. His cleaning of me is foreplay I didn't invite, but I love it.

I've never had this, whatever it is.

If someone asked me what our interlude was in this moment, the thing we're doing in the shower, I would say it was intimacy.

That realization speeds my heart, spilling anxiety into me like tea into a cup.

But I don't pull away as his index finger glides deep inside and his tongue laps and sucks at my clit.

I moan, and my hands move to his head, pressing him deeper against me. When his thumb once again finds my back opening, I'm ready and bear down on those seeking digits.

I explode around him, and a scream lodges in my throat.

I would have fallen if Lariat didn't catch me. A masculine chuckle of satisfaction wakes me from my daze.

"God, I love the way you look right now." Lariat kisses me softly on the lips.

He smells of sex, soap, and me, and it's hot—hotter than anything.

Dangerous.

"How do I look?" I murmur, softly touching his face.

He allows it but I notice a slight tightening of his eyes.

Lariat's back to guarded. "Happy," he answers in barely more than a whisper.

He walks us to the bedroom. "And how does that make you feel, Shane Dreyfus?" I ask softly.

Lariat lays me down on my bed, naked and mainly dry.

He prowls up beside me, running a hand from shin to shoulder, tucking my wet hair behind my ear. "Like I want to do it all again."

So God help me, we do.

8

LARIAT

I think my spine is digesting itself. That, and I don't want to leave Angel.

I've got it bad, inside of a goddamned day.

That's how I know I have to get the fuck out of here. I'm so bent on getting inside her, I didn't even check her house out first.

I left the fucking keys stuck in the lock.

Smooth, Lariat. Way to go.

Angel is asleep in my arms, her naked skin like porcelain against my naturally darker flesh. Her face is tucked against my shoulder, and inky lashes fan across her upper cheekbone, right where a large bruise spreads from the impact of a fist.

Just looking at that mar against her perfect skin makes my heartbeats pile up. I want to fuck Tommy up. Again.

Or anyone who would touch her.

I brush a single strand of hair off her temple, and she stirs but doesn't wake.

My smile is slight as I remember her lips on my cock, the way she made me come from my toenails. Again.

The possibility that I'm a cum machine occurs. I must manufacture the shit constantly. I lay a fist against my lips to keep the laugh in.

Angel moves fitfully, a little whimper coming out. I tuck her in tighter, and a slender arm extracts from between us, draping elegantly over my torso. A foreign emotion wells inside me, tightening my chest and hurting my fucking brain. It makes my teeth ache.

I want to wrap her in my protection—a girl I've fucked three times in the space of a day.

The thought sobers my lovestruck ass.

Carefully, I move out from underneath her arm and slide out of the sack. I gaze at her, naked and perfect.

I have to implement some self-preservation.

I scrub a hand over my skull trim. My exhale is exhausted. But I can't sleep. I wanted to look at Angel worse than I wanted shut-eye.

She slept, though. And I looked over the small abrasions and larger bruises on her body. I tried to be careful of her while we were sexing each other up. But Angel spurs a man on with her noises and sounds of pleasure. There's nothing I like more than hearing and seeing a chick get off. Nothing.

Unfortunately, I've liked it best of all with Angel.

I glance around her digs. Nice. Of course her space is nice in the high-end of Meridian Valley Country Club. The area is a long-time fancy gated community in Kent. It's a place that a young Shane Dreyfus would have loved to live inside. My old man did the best he could. Mom died when I was young, so all I had was Mini's dad and my own. And Mini.

Then Mini's dad died. We assumed Mini couldn't handle shit and got outta dodge, so to speak.

But now I know different because of Angel.

Life is funny that way. I find my cousin and this woman all at the same time.

The last twenty-four hours have turned my emotional baggage upside down. Forget about the suitcase of shit I've been lugging around for fucking years; it's the entire closet now. And it's ransacked.

Angel has made me feel, and that's why I have to establish some distance.

I back out of the room and softly shut the bedroom door. Turning, I grab my shit off the floor then hop into my jeans, dancing on one foot to put them on.

My eyes discover one sock on the back of the sofa, and I stifle a laugh. My shitkickers sit by the door on their sides like forgotten sentinels.

Jesus, what an idiot I am.

I get those on, tear on my T-shirt inside out, grab my cut off the back of the couch, and shrug it on.

I scoop the truck keys off the floor with my fist then open the front door and extract the house keys from the lock. I back up inside the house, lock the door from the inside, and quietly hang the keys on the key hook job I spot on the wall.

I silently shut the door, check that it's locked, and nod to myself as I walk toward the truck.

When I'm almost there, I turn and survey the house. The nice rambler probably has a walk-out basement. The stucco finish suggests it was maybe built in the 60s.

I pat the interior pocket of my cut, realize I gave up smoking four years ago when I separated, and heave a sigh. I park my ass against the truck, crossing my feet at the ankles, and take in Angel's place.

I hate leaving her alone, naked and vulnerable.

Maybe when I hand over that bail money tomorrow, I can con Noose into getting over here and doing some preliminary security detail.

Of course, that means admitting to him that I give a shit about something. And we're not on great terms. We could be if I just had it out with him.

But I don't know if I want to commit to that either. Heaving another raw exhale, I straighten and walk around the back of the pickup. I jerk the door open, hoist myself inside, then crank her over and roar out of there.

My head is filled with thoughts.

Thoughts of Angel.

I hear the truck start then rumble away from the curb, and I know Lariat has left.

I breathe a sigh of relief.

No matter how much I want Lariat—and I'm not so much a fool I can self-delude about him—we're not good for each other. We're from different backgrounds.

I'm thoughtful and conservative.

He's crude and violent.

But he was tender with me. The phrase whispers through my mind.

I flip the covers back and wince at how sore I am. I guess that's what I get for screwing three times in twenty-four hours and oh yeah, one time against a wall. *Good lord.*

Thank God I get the shot and don't have to worry about pregnancy.

I would be a terrible mom, what with the foster system as example. I shove the memories of that man far away.

Counseling gave me my life back, but sometimes, the body remembers that which we most wish to forget.

Why Lariat doesn't make my normal triggers rise, I don't know. He should. It could simply be that he saved me before anything happened between us. He breached one of the biggest barriers I have. What male has ever just protected me for its own sake?

None.

Until Lariat. He saw a man hurting me and couldn't abide it. When I couldn't deny our chemistry, I didn't try.

I stand, walk to the shower, and turn it on.

This time, I brush out my hair first and shampoo it twice. I rewash all my parts again, and that delicious soreness reminds me of how Lariat felt as he moved inside of me.

Powerful, tender, and constant.

I was so wrung out, I fell asleep with him beside me. Another first.

However, he and I have secrets. I can tell. A person who has horrors in her background can easily spot it in someone else.

I know Lariat has seen horrors. They might not be the same brand as mine, but they're still horrible.

I won't ask. I can't. If I try to get close to him, heal him of his wounds, then I have to revisit my own.

No fucking way.

I dry off and wrap my hair in a towel. Then I drape a robe on and cinch it tight.

I pad across my room, pluck my cell out of my now beat-up handbag, and Google the towing company.

Someone answers on a Sunday, thank God.

Do I know it'll be extra to change out the tires so my smart car will roll to the mechanics?

Yes.

Do I know it'll be double the hourly rate because it's a Sunday?

My shoulders tighten.

Yes, I answer.

If it was the good old days, I would slam the phone receiver down, but that's in the past. All I can do is tap the *end* button on my phone with an angry index jab.

My insurance company is going to *love* this.

I walk out into the living room and flop on the couch. Normally on a Sunday, I do some crafty thing. As a guilty pleasure, I like to refinish antique furniture or make glass beaded jewelry. But today, my body aches from getting tossed around, and my pussy throbs for one man.

Lariat.

A guy who took off after I swallowed his cum and shared the most intimate hours of my life with.

He snuck off like a thief in the night, without a good-bye or a piss-off.

He just left.

A single, scalding tear trails down my face, sliding between the neckline of my thick, terry cloth robe and pooling in the hollow of my collarbone.

Several more join the first until I'm actually crying. I cry in a way I haven't since that first time I was raped in my new foster home.

Somehow, this sadness is worse because the promise of happiness is lost. Whereas the terrible hurts of my past were always what they were—terrible. With Lariat, for a brief and shining moment, I allowed that crack in my armor to widen. He slid in when I was unguarded.

Lariat gave me hope.

Then stole it away.

So that's how I spend my Sunday, crying over what might have been and trying not to cry over what has already happened.

I jam the car into neutral and kill the engine. I hop out and jog into the new Road Kill digs. I love the old building Vipe finessed in here, bypassing the county fools and fucks, even letting the girlie greenhouse the old ladies insisted on happen. The place looks tight. And it is. Security was put in by Noose, and quadruple-checked by me, Wring, and Snare. It's airtight. If fuckers get in, they're like cockroaches—they ain't coming out. The thought makes me bark out a laugh because I'm thinking of the Bloods and the Tommys of this world.

I punch in the code and open the solid steel door then stroll through. It clanks closed behind me, and I survey the landscape.

Lots of half-naked chicks are sprawled out with some brothers, snoring and in various degrees of compromise. Bras, panties, and the stray cut are scattered around like lost leaves from a tree.

I kick a random boot as I walk by, enjoying a brother sitting straight up with a shock of hair on one side and a matted-down mess on the other.

Trainer sees it's me and gives me the stiff middle finger, one blurred and bloodshot eye zeroing in on my form.

Right back atchya. I lift my own salute, and with a grin, he flops back down, half on top of some skank-of-the-moment from Saturday night.

She yelps and jumps up. A nice set of tits jiggles around. One bra strap is looped on an arm, and the rest dangles like a forgotten flag of lace from her shoulder.

I snort. "Church in"—I glance down at my cell—"five minutes, Romeo."

Trainer jerks up again like a half-lit zombie. "Fuck!" he bellows

The sweet butt lurches up, tits swinging.

"Huh?" she asks in a daze then promptly falls on her ass, flashing pussy all over the club. Then she turns a little green around the edges.

Here we go.

The sweet butt upchucks between Trainer's legs.

Fuck me. "Nice," I drawl.

"Come fucking on!" Trainer roars, staggering to his feet, puke lacing the insides of his thighs.

I lift an eyebrow. "Look on the bright side, you got clothes on."

His bright hazel eyes latch on to me with clear irritation. "Oh yeah, so motherfucking funny, Lariat."

Totally hilarious. In fact, it gives me a funny bone that won't quit.

Of course, that lasts about one point five seconds when I remember I have to face Vipe and the brothers about stepping in the middle of a big pile of mob shit.

Yeah.

I turn away from Trainer, poor fuck, and walk to the back of the new building. Right next to Doc's office is our new official church meeting room.

I slap open the solid core wood door, and the guys are all there, except Trainer.

"Trainer will be here in a sec. He's got a little vomit detail to figure out."

Wring snorts, giving a rueful shake of his head. "Dumb fuck. Some shit never changes."

I nod. No denying that shit. Nobody on the Earth is a better dude than Trainer, but clever is not his middle name.

"Okay." Viper levels his pale baby blues on my ass and cracks the gavel. Hard.

Fuck.

My insides grumble again for food, loudly.

Noose raises an eyebrow. I usually eat up, so my growling stomach is noteworthy.

Gotta fuel my big ass.

Leaning forward on his elbows, Vipe begins, clearly ignoring my belly issue. "Great job on the last gun take. Really. Now that the Bloods are all scattered to the four corners of the Earth like the cockroaches they are—due to the last mess, courtesy of Wring—we've got a bigger slice of the pie." His watery gaze flows over the brothers, and everyone gives Viper attention. Not only is he the prez, but he's seen stuff. War. And he's got intuition to spare.

Wring tenses, hearing the reproach in the reference to how he saved a woman tapped to be a Blood whore for that particular nasty gang. The situation ended well, but it could have just as easily bitten the club in the ass.

Viper lets the comment swell and gain momentum then brings the machete down on my neck. "Now we got Lariat." He steeples his fingers, looking directly at me.

"I don't know what the fuck it is, but you boys can't seem to keep your finger outta the *get fucked* pie." He slaps his palms on the table.

His eyes are all for me.

"Lariat tells me his long-lost cousin has come out of the woodwork, and a fancy-schmancy lawyer reaches out, says, give me money to spring her, and you meet." He nods about ten times, rolling his lip inside his teeth and tapping his fingers on the polished wood tabletop. "Then wham!" he roars, and we all grimace as one. "She gets beat by a mob dick. Our brother Lariat gets a load of that noise and determines it won't happen on his watch." He turns his attention to me and raises his eyebrows.

"Yeah," I confirm cautiously.

He sweeps his palm toward me.

"He says yeah. "

I scowl.

"So he saves Miss Hot Pants Lawyer, and it's a twofer because Lariat saves her then gets the full motherfucking attention of the local mob."

Vipe begins clapping, and Trainer walks in right then.

He starts clapping too. "What are we clapping for?"

"Knock it off, ya mouth breather. Lariat's getting his ass chewed," Noose states helpfully.

I glare at Noose. "Thanks, ya dick."

His middle finger hikes. "Welcome."

"Boys," Vipe warns.

The silence swells. "Now, tell me this or forever hold your fucking peace. Is this all I need to know? You saved the lawyer broad, and she's in charge of getting…"

"Mini," I answer deftly.

He nods. "*Mini* outta the slammer for wasting Hubby?"

My silence is filled with lies by omission. "Yeah."

"Okay," Vipe says. "We'll deal with the mob fucks if it comes up. Thank fuck. For once, pussy isn't involved. That'd complicate shit to death." He swipes a hand over his salt-and-pepper, closely shorn hair.

His eyes sweep us. "Now, onto shit that matters."

Nooses's eyes travel my face. He smells a rat.

My palms dampen.

Yeah, it's me.

9

ANGEL

I give a last critical look at my reflection and sigh. Not much I can do with my face. It looks exactly like what it is:

A woman trying to cover up a beating with a skillful makeup job.

I wear a long maxi skirt today. There's no getting around it. I woke up this morning feeling even more beaten up than yesterday. My waistband is very close to the sight where Tommy kicked me. So I wear a looser skirt that's totally too casual for the office but won't make me wince every time I turn. I keep forgetting what bruised ribs feel like; it's been a while.

At least they're not broken.

I grit my teeth, dreading having to deal with Lariat again as I'll see him at the office first thing to collect bail.

Oh well, I have to pull up my big girl panties and deal. I straighten my fitted, dark-navy blouse, which perfectly sets off the exact color of the skirt, and slide my feet into ballet flats of the same tone. It's a very monochromatic look for me. The skirt barely clears the ground. I bought a tall size, so my clothes actually look good on me because they fit.

My eyes rise to my reflection again. The bruise is dark, but the furthest borders of the contusion are already starting to fade to yellow, like the edges of burning paper.

A honk blares, and I move to the door so I can peek out from behind the slatted wood blinds.

A glaring gold taxi waits. The exhaust is a reminder that autumn is here, but only in the mornings. By two o'clock, it'll be sixty-five degrees.

That's why I leave my coat and quickly lift another purse, one not trashed by the beating fun of Saturday, and carefully put it on my shoulder, mindful of my ribs. I open the door, lock it, and stuff my keys in the front pocket of my handbag.

I walk to the taxi and, for the first time, find myself warily searching the street, looking for Tommy or anyone like him.

I hop into the cab, and a guy with a greasy baseball cap meets my eyes in the rearview mirror.

"Where to?" He pops a series of bubbles that snap like firecrackers, and my shoulders tense. "Budget Car Rental," I answer evenly.

His olive-colored eyes flick to the rearview mirror. "Address?"

I answer, and Mr. Personality grunts a reply.

Five long minutes later, I arrive, pick up my rental car, and make arrangements with my insurance company as I drive to work.

By the time I hit the front door of my office, I'm in a foul mood. My face looks like shit, my body hurts whenever I turn, and I anticipate having to explain what happened about fifty-two and a half times.

Or at least I thought I did.

People are scrambling in the office. Maryanne, the firm's secretary, is racing around.

What the hell is happening?

She sees me and stops short. "Thank God," she groans, jogging over to me.

What now?

"I've been trying to reach you."

My phone is shattered from when I dropped my purse in the Tommy event, and I feel like an amputee without it. "I dropped my phone; it's broken." Probably the first of many white lies.

She nods, appearing to completely miss my messed-up face and casual outfit. "Your client..." Maryanne begins, her bottom lip trembling.

My body goes still. I currently have five clients, but only one that I care deeply for, that Maryanne would think to give this reaction about.

I stab out a guess. "Mini Dreyfus?"

Maryanne nods. "I'm so sorry."

I grab her arm, and she winces, as do I from the too-abrupt movement of my tender body.

"What?" My voice is a low roar. Blood whooshes in my ears, and the chaos of the room stops as three other attorneys look up at the same moment from various tasks of frantic conversing to phone calling.

Whenever a client is involved in violence, it turns the office upside down. We're all well-versed in each others clients cases. It's imperative for the smooth operation of the law office of Jugtner, Cognate, and Anderson.

"There was an incident at the jail."

"Involving her?" I ask stupidly. My hand floats to my throat as my lungs fill with fire. I realize I'm not breathing.

Maryanne nods, tears filling her eyes. "I'm so sorry," she repeats.

"Tell me." But my voice is listless to my own ears.

I already know.

"She's dead, Angela."

My vision grays at the edges, and I give a frantic look around, throwing my arms out. I manage to stagger over to a plush leather bench, which is deeply divided in diamond shapes and anchored by brass studs.

I fall into it.

My great whooping breaths sound like a suffocating siren in the office.

Hands grab me, and I bat them away. Someone notices my face and asks questions with a mouth that opens and closes, but I don't hear.

I. Can't.

Breathe.

"She's hyperventilating. Call an ambulance!"

No. No 911 for me.

That'll be on my record. And I hate hospitals. I didn't go for this beat-a-thon from Tommy, and I won't go now. They file reports.

Reports get you hurt. It's not a rational thought process, but it's one that is so real, I can't breathe past the thought of it.

My fingertips bite into the suede-like leather. The bulbous brass upholstery buttons heat under my hands as I concentrate on controlling my breathing.

It's your fault, Angel.

Wet heat drips down my face, and I cup my hand over my mouth.

I can't breathe. My limbs shake, and I start coughing as my body tries to overcome my mind.

"Get the fuck out of the way if you want to stay unbroken," a voice like rough gravel commands.

I swing my face in the direction of the arguing.

Oh no.

Vaguely, through the pinholes of my vision, Lariat appears. His eyes find me, and he shoves one of my colleagues. The man flies, landing hard on his ass and sliding a foot across the floor.

I stand, still can't suck breath, and fall back on the couch.

"What did you do to her?" Lariat roars.

My mouth is opening and closing like a fish out of water.

Nobody did anything. I just can't breathe because somehow, I'm responsible for his cousin's death.

"Nothing!" Maryanne tries to say.

But Lariat makes his way to me like a steam locomotive with a depot in sight.

He grips my shoulder.

"What's going on?" His eyes search my face. "Why aren't you breathing? Has someone hurt you?" His eyes canvas the room with jet-black poison.

I shake my head, a wheezing thread of oxygen trying to leak through my lips.

Lariat's eyes fall to my mouth, and he leans down. His lips are so close to mine that with a hard thought, they would land.

Then they do.

He startles me instantly, and I suck in a gasp, collecting oxygen like a starvation victim.

My fingertips curl on the edge of the patched leather vest he wears, and feeling returns. My face heats, and my breath comes in a whaling rush.

Lariat leans back, and my eyes widen as I look at a point behind his shoulder.

In an instant, he slams his elbow back, much more expertly than I'd done with Tommy. It lands hard, taking another male attorney out of the melee.

"Lariat," I choke. Then I groan as my ribs shriek at the demand caused by my rapid, deep inhales.

He spins, standing simultaneously. "Anybody feeling froggy? Gonna land on my lilypad? Go ahead." He literally beats his chest.

The other would-be saviors back away in the first smart move of the day.

Two male attorneys stay on the ground, looking up at him as if he has gone legitimately berserk.

Which is not a completely absurd thought.

"Angel, who is this?" Brad asks, delicately touching himself as though he's broken.

Brad is a consummate actor, as many of us need to be in court. I prefer not to pretend at every other moment of my life and resent his intrusion.

But I can't fault him. I had a meltdown, albeit warranted. My face is beaten up, and I just found out my client died in jail. Everything points to things not being okay. Brad was within his rights as a colleague to show concern.

Just the thought of Mini dying brings a fresh wave of tears.

I cover my face with my hands. In one fell swoop, I've managed to give every bad impression I can come up with to my coworkers. And that is on top of the disaster I survived and Mini's death.

"Did he do that to your face?" Brad asks, standing and glaring an accusation at Lariat.

An expression of disbelief washes over Lariat's face. "Should've stayed on your ass, pussy."

Oh my God.

I slap a palm on the wall and hoist myself to my feet, watching Maryanne dial 911. "Maryanne, put the phone down."

Her eyes widen, and she quickly shakes her head. Her eyes peg Lariat as if he's certifiable.

But not all things are as they appear.

"I have this under control." My voice only shakes a little, and I put my hand against my tender side.

Brad looks at me. His pale-blond good looks got him places that intelligence failed him. He would be wise to keep his mouth shut if he has any idea of what Lariat is or of the man's potential.

Of course, Brad doesn't. "Maryanne, disregard what Angel just said. This man's abused her, and she's obviously consenting, so get the police here now."

I walk toward Maryanne with every intention of grabbing that receiver and keeping this little disaster contained.

But then things go from bad to worse.

Brad reaches out to me, hooks an arm around my waist, and draws me close. I whimper from pain as his lips press against the shell of my ear. "He's dangerous. Stay with me until the police come."

Lariat's gaze takes in the hand around my waist, and he smiles. It's not a joyous smile; it's predatory.

My body tenses at his expression. "Let go, Brad."

"Absolutely not. He's deranged."

But Lariat is coming.

I rip out of Brad's hold and stumble Lariat's way. He begins to move around me, his eyes intent on Brad.

From behind, I wrap my arms around his waist, whipping against him from his momentum alone.

Lariat hesitates.

"Please," I whisper. "Don't."

His hands cover mine, and he holds me against him. "Who is this dickhead?" he grates.

My heart is trying to beat out of my chest. "My coworker. Another attorney."

"Who are you to investigate our relationship?" Brad interjects in his cultured voice as if he has the biggest death wish on Earth.

Shit.

Lariat gently sets me aside, walks two paces, and neatly punches Brad in the jaw as though he's swatting a fly with his fist.

Brad folds, and that's my cue to wilt on the spot. I cave to my knees on the floor.

This can't be happening.

Then the wail of sirens break up the fun. This is a real-life nightmare.

Maryanne comes beside me, kneeling. "Are you okay?" But her eyes stray to Lariat, who stands with his fists at his side, circling his neck as though he's trying to get the kinks out.

I nod quickly, gripping her hand. "Lariat doesn't know."

Maryanne's overly plucked brows come together in a snarl of confused flesh. "Lariat?"

"Shane Dreyfus."

Lariat looks at me as the cops start surrounding our building.

"That's Shane Dreyfus—the cousin?"

I nod.

"Oh boy." Maryanne's voice is disheartened. "Did he hurt you?" Her eyes cover every inch of my battered face.

I shake my head. "No. He helped me." *Saved me.*

Lariat meets my eyes. "I'm here to shell out the cash for the bail." His dark eyes narrow as he scans the knot of cops with their guns drawn, and he just as quickly dismisses them.

I'm out of my depth now.

I do remember that I was worried about seeing him before I got in the taxi. The thought is almost enough to keep the hysterical bubble of laughter contained.

But not quite.

How can I tell him Mini is dead? The cops flow in and start screaming that he needs to get down. His knees hit the polished marble floor.

I flow to my feet in a move so smooth that I surprise myself and apparently everyone else around me.

I go to Lariat. The cops shout at me to stay away, but I sink to my heels.

Lariat's hands are knotted behind his head. "Stay away, Angel," he says in a gentle but gruff tone.

"No," I whisper. I grab him, wrapping my arms around him as if he's the last solid thing in the world.

I've caused this mess, and now I have two people I'm responsible for.

I have to make this right somehow. "I'm so sorry," I whisper against his hair, which is still damp from a shower.

He gives me a one-armed hug. "Nothing to be sorry for, babe. Life's a crapshoot, and I won't be played."

I look up at him, shoving every bit of how confused, hurt, overwhelmed, and hopelessly gone over him I am into my gaze. "I'm not playing you."

"Neither am I."

"Hands fucking up!" screams a female cop.

Lariat unthreads his fingers, and his heavily muscled arms rise.

I stand. "He's okay!"

Lariat stands too, towering over me, and moves to lace his hands over his head again.

"Hands raised," a cop says, moving in.

Lariat complies, but I can't let go of him. Just an hour ago, I was counting my blessings that he wasn't with me.

"Ma'am, step away."

I hold on, my breath a stubborn ball inside my lungs. My heartbeats stall out.

"It's okay," Lariat says. "I'll be out inside of an hour. Babe, let go."

Maryanne touches my back, and I start as though I've just woken from a horribly vivid dream.

She extracts me from Lariat, and they swarm him like angry bees, bringing the giant of a man to his knees a second time.

I weep.

Brad smiles.

And something fragile inside me dies. I can't name what it is or why it's there, only that the loss of it suffocates me.

The police haul Lariat into a waiting squad car, and all I can think of is that he doesn't know Mini is dead.

And deep down, I know her death is my fault. Somehow, if I hadn't been involved, she would be alive.

Maryanne holds me while I ruin my careful makeup job. Every trace of the beating is revealed like painted wounds on my face.

10

LARIAT

I lied.

The club lawyer has me bailed out in about forty minutes. I told Angel it would be an hour.

I grunt. *Pudwackers.*

I probably shouldn't have tapped old Brad. It felt great, though. He was looking at me as though I was dog shit on the bottom of his shoe.

Pansy doesn't even know that I signed up to protect his right to be *him*. That ignorance must be bliss for the Brads of the world.

"Your relatively recent honorable discharge coupled with your decorated service made things easy, but Lariat..."

Our club lawyer pauses as I head out to the truck a prospect ran over here for me. I sigh as I take in the truck, missing my Harley. What I wouldn't give for the wind at my back and the ride between my thighs.

My exhale is harsh. "Yeah."

God, I want a smoke.

"You can't just go into an establishment such as that and start fist o cuffs."

I cock my head, barking out a laugh. "What kind of fucked-up expression is that?"

Al's lips thin. "What I'm saying is a bar fight can happen a hundred times, and Vincent won't need to pick up the phone. But one fight in a high-visibility law firm will do it every time."

Right. "Gotcha."

His earnest expression matches the eyes that search my face. "What were you thinking?"

That's the point. I wasn't. I just saw Angel's pinched, pale face and realized she was not breathing and that everything and everyone in that office was in some kind of uproar.

"Got involved in some class A bullshittery."

Al's wispy eyebrows rise, and I am reminded of how much he looks like an owl. Any second, I expect a hoot to plow through those thin lips.

Putting my hand on the door handle of the truck, I answer the unspoken question. "This is about my cousin, Mini. Chick at the law firm, Angela Monroe, is her lawyer. She got a hold of me, asking if I could front the bail." I lift a shoulder. "So I met up with her at Garcia's last Saturday."

I wait for a second, and Al nods. Clearly, he knows the place.

"Anyway, she shows, and things go all right. We agree to meet at her swank office today so I can make bail for Mini." I spread my arms. "Go to leave the joint, and she's getting the shit knocked outta her."

Now it's Al's turn to sigh. "By whom?"

"Mob lackey."

Al actually slides a palm over his face. Twice. "Local family?"

"Sounds like."

"And what did you, in your infinite wisdom, decide was the best course of action?"

I glare at him. "Kicked his ass. Don't like men who hurt women."

"I don't either, Mr. Dreyfus, but this introduces a many-layered problem."

"Yeah," I admit.

"We have a count of—"

"Fist o' cuffs."

A ghost of a smile hovers then drops. "Aggravated assault. If Mr. Devon does not drop charges, it could go far. After all, he is an attorney."

Well, damn. "I assumed he was hurting Angel."

His one eyebrow hikes again. "And who is she to you?"

"Nobody," I say defensively. Just a chick I fucked. Three times.

Yeah, I'll keep that small detail out of the convo for now.

"I make it my job to know everything I can about each club member. I know everything about you that has any record. Your family history, your time in the service, your accolades, medals, health record—I even know your IQ."

I go quiet. So did the navy. It was standard testing for SEALs. They can't have any dunce caps. I badly hold the snicker in.

"You're extremely bright, Mr. Dreyfus. Too bright to be caught up in this kind of affair. I can't say this to some of the brothers, as Vincent refers to his merry little band of bikers." His look is sharp, missing nothing.

I wouldn't refer to us that way, either. But then again, I don't talk like this mouthpiece, either. I hate that he knows all that shit about me, but I guess if he didn't, Al couldn't get us off the various hooks we hang ourselves on.

"You're not going to go and blab all your Lariat intel to everyone, are ya?"

He shakes his head. "I am only restating the facts. Not even from my perspective. Your father scored off the charts for spatial ability, mechanical, and mathematic aptitudes."

God, I need a smoke. I pat my pocket down and remember I've got a stale pack in the glove box. Ignoring Al, I jerk open the car door. It shrieks in protest. I twist the metal knob on the glove box, and it pops open.

Maps and a bunch of other papers and shit fly out. I grab the pack, tap it open, and clamp a cig between my lips.

I turn on the truck and smack the lighter hard.

"As did his son," Al says over the roar of the engine.

The lighter spouts out, and I press the glowing end to my cig. It ignites.

I drag deeply, feeling instantly better, and shoot the whole billowy mess into the sky. "So?" I ask.

Al crosses his arms, and I know when a man is getting ready to dig in his heels and make some kind of point. "Vincent needs you. You're the backbone of the club. You and Snare. He keeps guard, and you make sure the money is liquid and solid—legitimate."

I smirk. "You're saying I'm too valuable to spout off whenever the urge strikes?"

His expression is relieved. "That is precisely what I'm saying."

"Sorry, Al. No can do. Got a woman involved."

He looks pained. "There are over three billion women in the world, Mr. Dreyfus. Why must you choose the one woman that seems to have complicated circumstances surrounding her?"

I shrug. "Just lucky, I guess." Besides, I don't feel as though I've chosen anyone. I feel as if fate has just sort of chucked her in front of me, and I have to see it through.

"Think with your head, Mr. Dreyfus."

"Call me Lariat."

Al inclines his head. "Bail was easy this time, Lariat, because you've managed to fly under the radar, as the saying goes. Until now. But if you keep cropping up in the wrong places at the wrong times, it won't be easy at all. And those kinds of events will bring unwanted attention to Road Kill MC."

Al is putting me on notice. I fling the cig, and it lands on the asphalt outside the police station, smoldering. I grind it with the toe of my deeply treaded boots, killing the flame.

I walk into Al's space. Makes him nervous. He pushes his glasses up a skinny nose. His eyes are kind.

Vipe didn't hire a dickhead lawyer, but Al is smart, and he gave me the subtlest warning I've ever received. But I don't like it, based on principle.

"I hear you. But like I said, if someone is hurting a woman, I don't give a ripe fuck if it's the president of the United States. He's going down."

Al pinches the bridge of his nose. "Please try, Lariat."

I nod. I will. But it'll be for the club, not because of some lawyer who's scared I'll get a spotlight on us.

He begins to turn away then halts and slowly turns toward me. "There is another matter I almost don't wish to bring up, but because of the way you…handled some things, I feel as though more knowledge is better in your case."

I feel the scowl. I'm in no mood for riddles or other circumspect shit. "Spill it."

"Angela Monroe has a checkered past."

Really? I'm all ears. "Yeah?"

He slowly nods. "Juvenile records are normally closed."

I snort. "Not to a club lawyer."

Al shakes his head. "No," he says softly. "Sometimes, I follow a hunch up with a bit of green behind it."

I get his meaning. He paid someone off to break into sealed records.

"I wondered why a young woman, fairly fresh out of law school with seemingly everything before her, would be working pro bono, and on cases that seem to involve women almost exclusively. Women with certain backgrounds. There was a commonality there that couldn't be negated."

My heart starts to race. Instinctively, I know I'm not going to like whatever revelation Al is going to lay on me. I pluck another stale smoke out of the pack, crush the empty, hard-top box in my fist, and chuck the ball of trash in the back bed of the pickup.

The engine purrs at my back, and I hit the lighter again. It's hot almost instantly, and I light the tip of the smoke then shoot a stream into the air.

"Angel had a boyfriend that used his fists on her?" I take a second drag.

I suspected as much.

"No."

I come off the side of the truck I was leaning on. "What?" I realize I'm growling at him, and I try to chill, missing the mark by the width of the Grand Canyon.

"Her parents were killed when she was younger."

"How young?" I fucking know where this is going, and I don't want to hear it.

But I have to.

"Twelve."

"What happened?" I take another drag and hold it as though it's dope, deep in my lungs.

"Medical records show an ongoing trend of physical abuse."

I release the smoke in a boiling exhale. Sweat stings as it beads on my upper lip. "Sexual?"

Al dips his chin in a nod so subtle I would've missed it had I not been watching. "She was eventually removed from the home. Unfortunately, not before a great deal of trauma was meted."

Eventually.

I swipe my hand across my short hair. Fuck, fuck, *fuck.*

"I only tell you this so you know that you're not deal-ing with a whole woman. She's broken. Angela Monroe takes only cases where she can rescue a woman from a similar background."

"Angel thinks she's making a difference."

Al nods.

"Why does this matter to me?"

Al's eyes widen, and his palms spread away from his body. "I believed you could make clearer choices."

"You saying she's not worth defending because she's all fucked up?"

117

"No. I only meant"—Al's head hangs—"that the mob will know these things about her. Easily. They most certainly already do. The violence against Ms. Monroe will escalate as they seek more strident methods of persuasion or coercion. They want something from her, and your involvement endangers too much. Especially since, through our conversation, you've made it abundantly clear that you detest violence against women."

"Don't you?" I ask, letting the disbelief bleed through my voice.

He nods. "Yes. But I'm in no position to stumble across the scenario of a woman being beaten and do anything about it. I could have procured assistance. However, that particular finger of the mob would have done worse to me than what happened to Ms. Monroe."

We stare at each other. "You're saying walk away, let shit play out."

"I'm saying it *will* play out, with or without you as part of it. It would be prudent if you were not party."

"I don't know if I can do that, Al," I admit softly.

My memory helpfully conjures up Angel's face, the golden-emerald eyes, the soft black hair, and the freckles peppering the bridge of her nose.

I also think of the bruise from Tommy's fist.

Then I remember the sensation of my cock in her and how right she feels against my body.

Al studiously watches my expression. "I was afraid of that. Will you tell Vincent about the extra angle of your involvement, or shall I?"

My face whips to him. "Don't tell the prez nothing. I'll deal with it."

"I'll give you time, but my first loyalty is to Vincent."

"I know."

Al puts out his hand for me to shake, and I give it a hard pump. He winces but keeps hold.

He's a good guy; he just doesn't get the lure of pussy, especially pussy with potential.

11

ANGEL

"Angel, that guy's dangerous." Brad takes the ice pack away from his jaw, where an ugly, egg-sized knot is playing havoc with his GQ good looks.

"Yes, I'm aware." *So aware.*

"Then why are you defending him?"

We're sitting on the same leather couch where I had a panic attack to beat all the others. I thought I was done with those, but I guess not.

I give an exhausted sigh. "I'm sorry, Brad. It might be because I was in charge of the Dreyfus case, and now Mini Dreyfus is dead. And Shane Dreyfus is her cousin."

Brad touches my hand lightly. I give him my full attention, and I can admit he is handsome. And there's never been a lack of him trying to persuade me to date him, but I just never wanted to mix work and pleasure. That didn't seem to make any sense. And with the smell, feel, and taste of Lariat still on my body, I can't do whatever *this* is.

I pull away from his touch.

I can tell by his miffed expression that Brad takes my withdrawal the wrong way.

Which, of course, is the other part of the reason I wouldn't see him. He gets offended at any perception of rejection, probably because he hasn't had enough of it. Angela Monroe's indifference is a novelty, one he doesn't like.

Brad's eyes narrow, and I rush into the awkward silence to explain. "I met Lariat over the weekend in order to feel him out, see if the personal touch would get the bail money for Mini."

"*Lariat?*" His eyes flow over my face with judgment. "How personal?"

I flush to my roots, my scalp tingling as though he were witness to those few hours that Lariat owned my body.

My soul, my mind whispers.

"I see. You slept with him." A flutter in his swollen jaw makes an appearance.

"What a conclusion to jump to," I say in as neutral a voice as possible, not giving an inch. Brad doesn't deserve that information. "Not that it would be any business of yours who I slept with, Brad." I lower my voice, cognizant of the ears in the room. "We knew it wasn't going to work between us."

His smile is cold. "Because you didn't want to try."

I stand. "I'm sorry that Shane Dreyfus jumped to conclusions and punched you. I'm sorry that you and I aren't dating."

The hell with how loud I am.

He stands as well, looking down at me from his six-feet-two-inch frame, oblivious to the curious stares we're getting from the office staff. His lips curl into a cruel smile. "And I'm sorry that you'll bang anything with a dick."

I slap his unscathed cheek.

The strike manages to hurt my ribs, and my palm stings. "And I'm sorry you're too crude to breathe the same air as me."

I spin on my heel and walk out of the office, barely keeping the tears in check until I can leave.

How can I ever darken the doorstep of my office again, knowing that his assumptions have been spun into a web of gossip where we both work?

The cops took our statements, and mine was to the point. Lariat has the sympathy of the situation going for him because of Mini's death, but I just put him in jeopardy because Brad is within his rights to press charges. If he truly suspects that I slept with Lariat after denying him for the year that I've been with the law firm, Brad will see Lariat rot in a cell to spite me.

Let's just *heap* the guilt on. It's not bad enough that Mini is dead and the mob is after me, but I screwed her cousin in some kind of fit of hormonal excess then got him tossed into a holding cell because I can't control my emotions.

With a jerking suck of breath, I stride to my rental car and nearly rip the driver's side door off the hinges. I've got to get out of here right now.

I know what I need and head there. All they can do is listen.

But they hear me; I know they do.

Scenic Hill Cemetery looms large. It's one of the oldest in Kent, situated on the east hill, looking over the valley. Well, that's not entirely true. There's another cemetery, literally the oldest in Kent, but it's more of a homesteader's plot than anything. It's located on the opposite side of Kent, almost in Renton, the armpit town just to the north of us. Scenic is well-established too, just not full of settlers.

I drive underneath the wrought iron gate, its scrolling ebony framework peeling like an onion scorched by the sun. As predicted, the day has warmed up nicely. I had set aside the day to get the bail situation handled.

But it is turning into another day of grief.

I've had many.

I park my car at the small building where people go to meet with funeral directors. I no longer get panic attacks when I come here. It's been almost fifteen years now. I don't miss a week. I avoid the anniversary of my parents death but always come on their birthdays. I'd rather celebrate their life.

I get out of the rental, and my feet carry me with unerring accuracy to their plot. It's a combined headstone. They died on the same day, but not at the same moment.

My dad lingered for an entire ten hours.

They wouldn't let me be there for his last breath, but I was there for his last words.

I still hear his deep baritone ringing in my ears. "I love you so much," he'd said.

Photos are now the only things that keep my parents image sharp in my mind, yet his words echo in my brain.

When my foster dad—what a joke—when he raped and beat me, my real dad's voice was there.

Endure, Angel.

Survive, Angel.

I almost hadn't. I turn my wrists over to face a sky choked with clouds. The skin at the edges of my blouse cuffs show the proof of my grief. The magic of what plastic surgery could later erase almost completely.

Lots of women might think they want to end their life—I knew I did.

It was only then, at fourteen years old and after two hard years of suffering, that I finally did what I had to do.

If I had to live another day in fear and self-loathing, I would rather not breathe.

So I didn't.

I sliced my wrists in the bathtub and let the water ease me toward death.

When I was found, it was almost too late.

Arnold would have let me die and gotten himself another innocent girl to decimate, but his wife, who'd never given a shit about me except for that state check, had called the ambulance. Guess my death would have been messier for them.

Child Protective Services removed me from the home, and I got well. I got strong.

I took self-defense classes so it wouldn't be easy for the next man to hurt me.

That's why Lariat is so wrong for me on the deepest of all levels. He's everything I should be afraid of—violent, gang biker, military assassin.

I cover my mouth with my fist. He's the beater of Brad.

Then the laugh explodes out of me anyway over my parents' grave. My smile fades, but the spoils of the humor don't, and my lips continue to twitch.

It feels good to have a little happiness, even at Brad's expense.

I run my fingertips over the smooth, cold granite where my parents' names are etched.

Libby and Gregory Monroe, Loving parents of their Angel.

I try not to let the memories surface. But they do, and I'm helpless in a current within the ocean of my grief.

I come here to this place and invite the fabric of my life to replay itself when I visit their gravesite.

"Angel," Mom says and rubs her thumb over the tip of my nose.

I sneeze, and flour blasts everywhere.

Her dark brown eyebrows rise. "You have more flour on your face than in the cookie dough."

I nod happily. "And I want to taste it before we bake it."

"It has raw eggs, Angel."

I giggle. "But you told me that you *always had the uncooked dough." I feel my eyebrows pop.*

Mom frowns. "Yes, I lived," she says with an abrupt chuckle. "But we did all kinds of crazy things when we were young. Rode in the back of pickup trucks, drank from the hose."

I pull a face of disgust. "Gross."

Mom gives a sage nod. "Yes, and we only had half a dozen channels for TV."

"I'd die," I breathe in horror, swiping some cookie dough when Mom turns her back to wash her hands.

"*Most certainly.*" *Mom's lips twist into a wry smile as she glances at me over her shoulder.*

Dad crashes through the door, full of energy and vitality as always. "What are my two favorite girls doing?"

Mom blushes, and Dad swoops in, giving her a kiss on the cheek.

My wooden spoon lands upside down in the batter.

"*Making you fat!*" *I yell, hopping off the counter and running to him. I wrap my small arms around his flat middle, and he smiles down at me, stroking the back of my head. "You can't make Daddy fat, princess. I do too much running around."*

My brows come together at our familiar verbal game, and I pull away, gazing up into bright hazel eyes, a perfect meld of gold and amber. "After who?" I shout, knowing the answer.

"*The crooks, of course!*" *he yells.*

I spin and run through the house.

Daddy chases me.

A few years after that early memory, they're dead.

I clench my eyes shut, driving the memory back underneath the steel of my skin.

Gregory Monroe was a defense lawyer. Mom made a hell of a batch of cookies, and she kept the house a home.

Tears stream down my face in burning, twisting rivulets of anguish.

"I hope you're proud of me, Daddy," I whisper brokenly. "Because I'm barely hanging on. One of my clients died, and I couldn't save her. I saved me, but I couldn't save her."

There's no comment from the grave, but my hand lies flat on their gravestone. The stone gradually grows warm beneath my skin.

"I've met a man." I bite my lip. "I don't know if you'd approve. But he saved me. He's so like you, Daddy. Not polished and classy, but truthful, brash, and gentle."

I don't think Lariat would appreciate my commentary. I swipe my eyes with my free hand, unwilling to break contact with the stone marker.

It doesn't matter what I say here. It's sacred. This is my communion with my dead parents, and I say everything to them.

"I miss you, Mama." I hiccup back my next words then finally get the nerve to tell them my most desperate wish. "I want what you and Daddy had. But I can't find him, Mama. I look, but all I see is the bad in humanity."

I tip my face to the sky, and a ray of early afternoon sun breaks through the clouds, hitting my face. The swelling has gone down, and the tender spot on my cheekbone welcomes the heat.

I lay the uninjured side of my face on their gravestone, cradling my head between my folded arms.

"I need something to feel happy about, like my life has meant something. Without you in it, I don't know what's left," I whisper.

That's not entirely true. I have a good friend, Trudie. But I can't tell her the entire truth—that I maintain distance from men and from loving someone because there has been no man I can trust since my dad died.

Though she might guess. Nor do I relish the eventual disclosure of my sordid past, which would eventually come up with friendships. I keep myself to myself.

It's not every day that a high-profile lawyer and his wife die in a gruesome car wreck. Then their orphan tries to commit suicide because the system failed, placing her with a sadistic rapist.

My identity was sealed by the courts, but the media can say everything but the identity of a minor. After a few days, everyone knew it was me. The town wasn't big enough to protect my anonymity.

One atrocity on top of another.

The fragile psyche of a child is always second to sensationalizing the next journalistic ladder rung.

The sun heats my back as I lie close to my parents. They're dead. I know this. But for a few minutes, I can be close to them. They loved me, and that knowledge is the solitary thing that has gotten me as far as I am today.

I only close my eyes for a second, but I should have known my exhaustion would take over.

12

LARIAT

"What the *fuck*?" Viper practically spits in my face.

I know I deserve his wrath, but I'm hot-blooded enough that the urge to knock his teeth down his throat surfaces like oil on water.

There's something to being a man who defaults to violence first that makes that part of him instantly accessible forever.

"I know I fucked up."

"Fucked up? Fucked up, he says!" Viper strides around the room we meet for church yesterday in a full-on lather. I expect him to froth at the mouth any second and tear out hair too short to yank.

He pivots, hands going to his lean hips. He's still in pretty good shape for a guy past fifty. There's nothing soft about Vipe. He's a fucking hard man, all five feet ten, steel hair, and piercing pale blue eyes of him.

That is probably why he has lasted as prez of the Road Kill MC for as long as he has—going on two decades now.

"It's gotten fucking complicated. I saved Angel—"

"Angel? Who?" Thick black brows edged in steel slump hard over his eyes.

"The lawyer, Angela Monroe."

He snorts, crossing his arms and giving a hard lift of his chin.

"Anyway"—I raze a palm over my scalp, feeling the short hairs of my flattop bristle against my calloused hand—"I slept with her."

"God *damn*!" Viper roars, a vein in his forehead standing at stark attention. "I *knew* this was about pussy. Holy shit in a sack." He beats his fist on the solid wood table carved with the Road Kill insignia and rests his folded knuckles against the polished wood surface. "Smell some pussy, hear it getting fucked, have a brother go all pear-shaped in his goddamned head…and sure as shit—*voilà*—there's a woman involved."

Couldn't fault his logic. "It didn't begin like that."

"No?" His eyebrow shoots up, and Wring snorts.

I send a glare his way that clearly conveys my message—*stay the fuck out of it.*

That just makes the bastard grin.

Fucker.

"Explain why my perfect, cool-as-a-goddamned-cucumber bean counter is hot in the trousers for some high-end tail mouthpiece."

"That's a helluva lot of words, Prez," Noose comments dryly. His thumbs are hooked through his belt loops, and one boot is planted on the wall behind him.

Wring grunts, cleaning his nails with a switchblade.

I roll my eyes heavenward.

"Fuck it!" Vipe roars, slamming his fist down again.

"I don't know," I admit in a low voice. "Don't give any fucks about tail. Sweet butts and club whores, they're easy pickings."

"Then explain this bit of fuckery," Vipe huffs, flipping a palm away from his body and slapping it back to place on his bicep.

"You gonna live?" Snare inquires from the group at Vipe, flipping his lighter open and closed.

Click. Snap. Click.

Vipe turns to him, incinerating Snare with a look.

"Fine, fuck," Snare growls. "You're not so fucking old that you can't remember a broad nailing you between the eyes, can ya?"

Vipe stands there, stewing, then finally begins to nod slowly. He puts his thumb and index finger so close together, air wouldn't fit. "Barely. And my old lady died ten years ago. Never gonna be another to replace that sweet bitch."

No shit. Vipe has near-shrine acclaim for her.

The brothers are smart enough not to say anything. A person doesn't talk about brothers old ladies in any way except *nicely* and live.

"So Al has to bail you out of a cell—loved getting that motherfucking phone call, by the way—because you went down to post your cousin's bail. But instead of just paying it all quiet-like, you fucking socked some douche mouthpiece right in the kisser."

That about sums things up. I hang my head. "Angel was doing some kind of cry fest and wasn't breathing, and that fucker was looming over her. Thought he was the cause of it."

"Didn't ask any questions, just charged in like an insane asylum candidate and introduced him to left and right."

I held up my fists, displaying a slight abrasion marring my dominant hand's knuckles. "Only right."

"Well, thank fuck for small miracles," Vipe says, clearly unconvinced.

Noose barks out a laugh, flopping on a nearby chair. He tosses his shitkickers up on the table, crossing them at the ankle.

We glare at each other over the toe of his black boots.

"I don't care if Lariat sticks his dick in a dog."

We all turn to Trainer.

He grins.

Wow. I stand, fists curling in readiness.

He holds up a palm to ward off the ass-kicking I've got planned. "Not finished. God, you guys are all fucking nuclear reactors." His gaze touches on Wring, Noose, and me—saving Snare for last. Our master-at-arms didn't serve with us, but he's been on the front lines ever since, so to speak.

"I'm just saying." He shrugs. "What's the big fucking deal over Lariat getting some fancy pussy?"

"Trainer, it's a miracle you patched in, and God only knows you've done your fucking time," Vipe begins. The good-natured chuckles that follow cause Trainer to scowl. "But it's not the *kind* of tail Lariat is tapping; it's that what he's tapped is mob-sanctioned."

Trainer's eyes take on that glazed look we all know so well.

Christ on a crutch. "Angel put away the local godfather, and now he's after anyone associated with his lockup. Only witness has already been axed." I spread my arms wide, letting the innuendo sit there. "In witness protection, no less."

"Heard he was hanging around by his guts," Wring comments in a Sahara desert voice, his glacial eyes rising to meet Viper's gaze.

He and Noose fist bump.

It would take a little more than some intestine swinging to get my former SEAL teammates riled—a hell of a lot more.

"What a colossal mess," Vipe says then jerks his chin up. "What about your cousin?"

I shrug. "I've got the money— bout cleaned me out. Took a whole year of running guns after getting my share to get that change. Now it's going to her. But"—I swipe my hand over my face—"she won't ditch the bail. Maybe Angel's even good enough at her job that Mini might get free. God knows if I'd been aware—"

"Husband was a cowardly fuck," Snare interjects, and I know he's thinking of his dad kicking the shit out of him. His old lady too.

"Juries are sympathetic to that shit," Storm says, entering the conversation for the first time.

I glance at him, giving an imperceptible nod. *True.*

"Now we have to be on point for these mafia bastards to show up and cause trouble. Because as sure as I'm standing here, they will." Viper is pissed at me and rightfully so.

I didn't come clean about Angel, but I didn't think it would matter. I still fucked with the mafia snake by beating on that little simp, Tommy. I can't take that shit back and don't want to.

Me having sex with Angel just deepens the mess, but it's still not enough to warrant the mafia snooping around, if—*if*—I was to walk away now.

But I can't. It's as if Angel's a magnet, and I'm slowly being drawn toward her.

"Hello." Vipe snaps his fingers in front of my face, and I come back to myself, embarrassed as fuck.

"Thinking about pussy. Wipes the brain," Snare says unhelpfully. "Never thought our boy Lariat would become a worshiper."

Noose snorts. "Knew he'd cave eventually."

We stare at each other again, and I have the certain knowledge that the shit between us has to get figured out. And I can see by his expression that he knows it too.

"We got your back, Lariat. But not coming clean with this bullshit surrounding how you felt about this girl wasn't good."

And *fuck*. "There's more," I admit.

"What could be worse than this cluster of a fuck?" Vipe isn't shouting. Yet.

I glance at Vipe, then my gaze travels the room. The men lean forward, tense.

"This goes nowhere, and in fact, I hate saying personal shit I don't own."

My SEAL teammates know what it is to confess. We don't do it unless it's a means to an end—an important one.

"Al—"

"Club lawyer?" Trainer interrupts.

I nod, getting back to grinding through the gist of it.

"He says that he looks into everything to do with the club. Bastard knows my IQ, nationality, former rank, and every little pat on my ass I received in the service. And that's the tip of the intel iceberg."

Noose's dark-blond eyebrows pop, and he slides his jaw back and forth. "Really? I'll be damned."

"He's a thorough little mole," Viper muses. "But what does that have to do with anything?" He lifts his shoulders, arms still folded against his chest.

"Angela Monroe's got history. Abused woman history."

Snare meets my eyes.

"That why she takes all these free cases as public defender?" he guesses with uncanny accuracy, getting to the meat of the thing.

I nod. "I figure."

"Did ya know?" Noose asks softly.

My smile is slanted, insincere.

"Yeah."

"You chumps just *gotta* get complicated pussy. Every one of you. It's like a theme." Viper shakes his head. "Goddamned lawyer. Obviously, she's smart. Not gonna just bang some biker guy, cuz she can have a rich prick any minute she crooks her finger. But oh *no*. She's gotta have a former Navy SEAL badass, whose hands are lethal weapons, and who holds the beans for the club. Further, she's gotta be mixed up in mob bullshit up the kazoo and have a relative of yours waiting in the wings who needs rescuing too. Perfect. I couldn't make this shit up."

"Sounds kinda bad when you say it like that," Trainer announces.

We turn our collective attention his way.

"It *is* bad, dumb fuck!" Viper breathes through his anger, hands fisted. "All right, ranting won't turn back the clock, but *damn* if it doesn't feel good. You"—he points at Noose—"get a prospect on this lawyer's ass because she holds the reins to a brother's family member."

"Mini's the only family I got," I confess.

Viper gives a solemn nod. "I know, and I'm cutting you some slack for not playing father confessor and just telling us you were tapping this girl."

My shoulders stiffen. "So when do I have to give you the names and phone numbers of every chick I bang?" I'm getting nice and pissed now, a fine clear rage veiling my vision like an opaque layer of red paint.

His intense eyes land on me and stay. "You don't, Lariat. Except when your conduct interferes with club safety because you're not *just* banging her. You give a shit."

And that's it, isn't it? I care. There's no denying it.

Snare stands, eyeballing me with intense blue eyes. "For the record, as master-at-arms, I sure would have liked the inside info that you just pounded the fuck out of Mob Boy then banged the chick they fingered. Further, you want a repeat performance, right?" His black hair contrasts with that sapphire gaze, seeming to make his eyes stand out like jewels in his face—hostile ones.

"Yeah, fuck." I scrape my palm over my face, pegging my hands on my hips and blowing a rough exhale out like a cannon fired. "Thought I could deal."

"You can't when emotional shit's involved. There's Mini, and now there's this broad." Wring looks at me with a question in his eyes.

"She's not a broad," I say through my teeth.

Wring's grin widens. "See? If she was twat-of-the-week, you'd shrug that comment off. But Angel's not, is she?"

They all stare, waiting for my response, and I don't drop my eyes. "I'm not saying she's old lady material or that I'm throwing down for her, got it?" I glare around the room in a clear challenge.

"But you're not saying she's *not,* and you *won't,* are you?" Vipe asks quietly.

No, I wasn't.

Fuck.

"Fucking smooth back there, Lariat," Noose begins without preamble as soon as we clear the door to the club.

Fuck. Knew it.

I whirl on him, and he clamps his teeth on his cig, crouching with a shit-eating grin. "Bring it, fucker." Smoke spirals upward as we square off.

I *want* to bring it. Even though I realize in a deepdown space I don't visit much that I'm unraveling and Noose is the target simply because of proximity.

I straighten, handling my shit. "No. Not gonna make you my punching bag."

Noose snorts. "Fuck off, you couldn't make me dick if you wanted to."

Jesus.

I turn to punch him, and Wring is just there, hand to my chest. "Cool it."

My chest heaves against his palm, and Noose looks over his shoulder, mirth in his eyes.

I sort of want to kill him.

"Noose, fuck off with the look," Wring says without turning.

"What—me?" His voice is all mock-innocence.

"I know you're making your lame faces behind my back," Wring says slowly.

A smoke ring rises in the air, and Noose takes another drag. "You're no fucking fun."

"So when has any of this shit been fun?" Snare asks, breaking the tension as he joins the lineup of us moving toward our rides.

They sparkle like simmering jewels in the late after-noon sun. Wring's has a custom candy-apple-red paint job, Noose's is jet black, and Snare's and mine are also black.

"Got a bad feeling about this one," Noose says out of nowhere.

I don't like the sentiment. He has the instincts of a psychic.

I turn to Snare in half-apology, regret seeping into my tone. "Didn't mean to jack you around."

He lifts a palm. "Fuck it. I know now. Would it have made any difference if I'd known before this lawyer got her ass kicked?"

I shake my head. "Hell no, that pencil dick needed a knockdown. Nothing would've stopped that from going down."

Snare nods soberly. "There's not anything anyone could do or say that would keep me from beating the fuck outta a man who laid hands on a woman." His shrug says *simple*.

Fists bump all around. "They're for fucking, not beating." Snare is thoughtful, his gaze a million miles away.

"And a little more than that," Wring adds with a wink.

"I didn't mean nothing by it," Snare says. "I love Sarah. My kid."

"I love Rose, Aria," Noose says.

"Are you guys all growing girl parts?" I ask in a gruff voice.

Noose opens his fly and checks out his junk. "Nope, still got a cock. Use it pretty often. Works awesome."

Wring snorts. "Think what our brother is saying is we never hated women. We're worshipers of their goods."

"Amen," I say, and the guys echo my sentiment.

"It's just, before the old ladies, my life was just fine worshipping from afar." Wring chuckles.

Snare frowns. "Getting poetic. Fucking chill."

"You're the college boy," I remind him.

He throws his hands up with a laugh. "Guilty."

Wring lifts a broad shoulder. "Then Shannon came along, and that distance bullshit wasn't good enough anymore. I wanted, for the first fucking time, up close and personal."

The silence is thick.

"True dat," Snare says thoughtfully then adds, "I wouldn't go back to those days."

"It was fun," Noose muses.

I nod. "It is fun." I get an image of Angel underneath me, inky hair spread out like a silky fan as I go deep, her half-closed eyes molten gold and filled with satisfaction. "But this is real."

Wring snaps his fingers and points at me. "That's what I mean. It feels like I'm living now instead of existing. I fucking sleep, finally," he says, almost as a tack-on comment.

We share a look. The guys have said that PTSD shit we've all been saddled with since the war is a fuck-ton better since they settled with their women.

I don't hold out hope for that. But I can do what feels real.

Angel's real.

13

ANGEL

Initially, it's the cold that wakes me up.

My disorientation is complete as I struggle to the surface, groaning at the stiffness in my ribs, face, and arms that have fallen asleep.

Scooping myself off the hard granite marker, I come to myself in jagged pieces of consciousness.

I take in the view of the cemetery and realize I fell asleep on my parents grave.

Soft light pools along the ribbon of asphalt pathways that wind their way between people's bodies and the memories they hold.

Blinking, I sit up straighter as feeling returns in a clumsy surge of pins and needles. I shake my hands out. The movement tweaks my ribs, and I groan.

Rubbing my bare arms, I move to stand up, sort of sway, and realize I haven't eaten a thing since my yogurt and peanut butter toast this morning.

I missed work and came here. I cover my face with my hands, pacing my breathing. I didn't tell Lariat about Mini.

Unforgivable.

My selfishness will hurt people more than my failure has.

Finally, I lower my hands, excusing myself from my own pity party.

It's time to face Lariat. I need to see if I can tuck my tail between my legs and kiss up to Brad so he won't press charges and make things worse for the man who saved me, just lost his cousin—and with whom I had the best sex of my life

Twilight seeps its dying light through the vagueness of the remaining leaves on the overhead trees. The red, gold, and orange leaves are licks of flames overhead as the last rays of the sun brush them to life.

I pull the ends of my navy cotton blouse down and roll my shoulders to ease the tension as I scan the cemetery a second time. I spot the rental sports car several yards away at the bottom of the gentle knoll where my parents lay and walk slowly toward it.

Before I've gone halfway, I glance back at their grave. Sucking in a breath, I let the fortitude from being here fill me with borrowed strength, their silent affirmation building me back up.

Giving them my back and walking away is always the hardest part of my visit. Away from them and my memories.

I want to forget I was ever part of a loving family. It would make what happened after their deaths so much easier to reconcile.

If all I'd known was abuse, then I would be none the wiser. But I hadn't. My dad had been a local celebrity, getting people off that deserved it and prosecuting people who were criminals.

My mom had been there as some kind of constant, warm presence that I had come to expect and rely on.

I don't allow the panic of their deaths to consume me anymore, but it's not without cost.

Instead, I stand in the middle of a graveyard that has gone dim from day's end. Chill bites at the edges of my warmth, stealing it as I relearn how to breathe. I narrowly stave off the well of feelings threatening to drown me.

Hopelessness and despair claw their way up my throat, and I physically demand my body to stop the regurgitation of the past.

In. Out. In. Out. Scalding breaths leap to the surface, burning my mouth with the heat of my memories. Regret and guilt war inside my gut. I lay a hand over my flat stomach, and a painful rumble ensues as though my body just realized how offended it is without fuel.

Movement causes my head to turn, and a figure trembles at the edges of my watery vision.

I rapidly blink, squinting and thinking briefly that this is a weird time for anyone to be at a cemetery. Nighttime isn't popular in graveyards. And most visitors don't fall asleep on graves. I can't make the person out perfectly as he hovers at the edge of the forest that borders the cemetery.

Better get to my car.

Gooseflesh slides over my bare arms as I stride to my borrowed vehicle and reach for the handle.

I don't see anyone as I travel the handful of yards to the car.

Breathing a sigh of relief and having the key fob at the ready, I hit the button to unlock the car.

A soft beep whistles in the still night, signaling that the car is unlocked.

I feel a presence like a weight at my back. The hairs at my nape rise, and I whirl around.

Tommy is a foot away from me. I have one conscious moment of recognition, taking in the strip of tape running crossways over the bridge of his nose. Even in the near dark, I can see that the skin underneath his eyes is shadowed by bruises.

Dropping my purse from my left hand and using the flat of my palm, I hit him hard in the nose Lariat clearly broke.

Tommy grunts from the impact but doesn't go down. Instead, his hand wraps around my throat and squeezes.

I cross my forearms and strike wide. Breaking the contact, I suck in a breath, choke on the pain, and lift my knee. I narrowly graze his crotch instead of achieving the direct hit I was going for, hampered by my long skirt.

He bends over at the waist, and I palm the back of his skull, slamming his face into the same knee.

Tommy leans sideways and falls over like a tree sawed in half. I sidestep his flailing arms and turn.

His shuddering, wheezing breaths fill the quiet.

My eyes dart around the manicured grounds, and I see more men walking slowly across the rolling lawn.

Oh my God.

These are men I know, men who watched their mob boss go down, men whose eyes ran over my body in clear lust and anger when I directed the jury to the truth. Justice was delivered by a woman who no doubt looked as though she wasn't smart and couldn't hold her own.

But life had honed me. My foster father's abuse had fashioned a steel center, and genes had dealt me an intelligent hand.

However, as the knot of four men draw closer, I realize there's no amount of smarts that will get me out of this.

I calmly snatch my purse from the ground, reach inside, and pull the .380 Beretta out. I train it on the man closest to me.

The whites of his eyes grow larger in the gloom of a night almost claimed by complete darkness. This far from the valley, the light pollution is held at bay, and the only thing to ensure illumination is the feeble light cast by the streetlamps.

He puts out his hands in a benign gesture that I know is as false as his appearance here. "Tommy was just going to talk to you, Angela. I swear it."

Right. Because he did so much *talking* the other night. "You don't know me well enough to address me by my first name."

His smile is predatory. "You wouldn't be much without your little gun, Angela." He bites my name off like a delectable morsel of food.

"You're an overly familiar prick, and I think I did just fine with Tommy here."

Tommy is busy groaning on the ground, his nose a pancake of ruined flesh.

The man's smile fades, and he jerks his chin at two of the three men flanking him.

"We thought Tommy would be enough of a warning, Angela."

I try to split my attention between him and the other three. "I did my job. Antonio Ricci is where he belongs."

He frowns, cocking his head to the right. "And *you* will be under our new regime. The boss wants you, Angela. And what he wants, he gets."

I shake my head, and I have another surge of light-headedness. *Go figure.* It's probably from the beatings, revelations, and lack of food.

"Just like he wanted your father."

My stomach bottoms out, right there. The nose of my pistol dips.

Sudden movement on my right has me pointing and shooting simultaneously.

Grass burps out of the ground in a small eruption, dirt flying as the report claps my ears with ringing pain.

A hand chops at the forearm of my gun hand, and my muscles spasm, releasing the weapon automatically.

Fuck. I duck, turning and plunging my left fist into the guy's nutsack.

He falls, and I stand, arms loose and ready. The element of surprise is long gone, and there are still three men to deal with. Tommy is recovering, despite the red ruin of his face, and the man I struck is on his knees, gasping for air.

He starts throwing up, and I sidestep the mess without taking my eyes off the man who keeps talking—trying to distract me.

His eyes fall on his men on the ground. "You're full of surprises, Angela."

I don't know this man's name. I knew Tommy because he introduced himself the first time he popped out of a dim corner to threaten me.

"I'm not doing anything for Ricci. I put him in jail. I'm an attorney, not a mob slut." My voice shakes, not with my conviction—though that's in there—but with fear.

"She's somebody's slut," one of the men five feet to my left drawls with rich sarcasm.

Giving him my attention is a luxury I can't afford. My gun is on the ground. If I make a move to retrieve it, I'll never get it in time. They'll be on me.

I have no chance against three men. None.

The realization makes my palms dampen enough that I don't think I *could* hold my gun.

The roar of bikes shatters the silence. At first, it's only a rumble of gravelly music in the distance, but it gains volume as the noise draws nearer.

The mob enforcers look toward the sound of approaching engines. Loud pipes sing their melody into the air, making the night vibrate.

The lead man scowls in that direction. "Grab Tommy and Aaron."

I flatten my palms against my car, and my heart beats a frantic rhythm as I inch down the side. My eyes are trained on the guy calling the shots.

He steps forward.

"Tell me why you mentioned my father. He's dead; he's been dead for fifteen years."

We face off just three yards from each other.

The sound of the bikes grows.

"He didn't do what he was told, Angela." His voice is smooth, low—convincing.

I'm *not* convinced.

"Did you wonder why we didn't have guns on you?"

I had.

"We don't want you dead. We just *want* you. Can't kill you, so we'll do the next best thing."

Headlamps blaze near the entrance. The other mob guys have managed to drag Tommy and Busted Balls away to the forest border.

"We'll be in touch, Angela," Talker says, backing up.

"My father—" I begin then bite my lip. Do I want to know?

Yes. "Your innuendos aren't going to win me over to whatever demented plan you have."

Talker winks. "But torture will do what everything else has failed at."

Then he's gone as the first of the bikes purr up beside my car.

Lariat's eyes meet mine, and several things hit me at once. I care for him when I shouldn't—*really* care. Which changes everything, doesn't it?

And how did he find me?

The last thing I'm certain of is that he has found out about Mini. It's in the set of his broad shoulders and the tightness around his eyes. His face contains a clear, pure rage that no lack of light can contain.

But more than that, his gaze travels the dark, shadowed corners of the cemetery, then comes to me again.

"Who the fuck was just here, Angel?" he growls.

How does he know anyone was here? They've gone like apparitions on the wind.

My heartbeats cram into my throat, and I find myself fighting yet another panic attack—because Lariat is coming toward me and I'm scared again…and exhausted.

I can't handle one more thing on my plate.

The ups and downs of my life's emotional roller coaster have me tangled, while deep inside, a small part of me unravels.

Questions crowd my already cluttered brain.

What does Antonio Ricci want from his prison cell? How was my father connected to him before he died?

Why is he having me beaten up one second then trying to get me to discuss an *arrangement* the next?

I don't answer Lariat's question. Our eyes lock in silent combat. He is in my personal space, so close I couldn't slide a sheet of paper between us. He's so tall, I crane my neck back to look up at him as the cool metal of the rental presses against the back of my thin blouse.

I shiver from the cold and from Lariat's boiling presence.

"You didn't tell me." His voice is low, careful.

I shake my head, relieved he doesn't question me further. "I should have."

"Yeah." He cups my chin with his strong hand. "You should've."

We stare at each other, and tears fill my eyes, making my vision shimmer. "I'm so sorry," I say in an agonized whisper. Nobody wants Mini alive more than me.

Lariat wraps his arms around me, crushing my face against his chest as my sadness soaks his leather vest.

"Nah, babe, don't take this on. You didn't kill Mini."

"I did," I vehemently deny. "I didn't get her bail figured out fast enough. I didn't petition for extra protection."

He props my chin up again, his thumb closing my lips. He searches my face as though he's counting my pores.

I become aware in excruciatingly slow moments that we're not alone. I need to come clean about what happened with Ricci's mob goon squad moments before—the men he already sensed had been here.

But I can't speak as Lariat strokes the side of my face with his thumb. I am transfixed by his presence and his gaze.

"I can help you, like you tried to help Mini, but I need you to do something for me, Angel."

I don't like owing anyone anything. I keep my own counsel. I've been doing it my whole adult life. "It depends," I reply carefully. "I don't want to make things worse for you."

Lariat's smile is a twist of lips. "Babe, I've got broad shoulders. I can handle it, trust me."

I take a deep breath, sort of half-collapsing against the car, and his palms go to either side of my shoulders, caging me in.

"What do I need to do?" I'm already in so deep, and in ways I can't extricate myself from.

"I need you to be my property."

My mouth gapes. "No way."

I'm never going to be owned by any man. My foster dad couldn't do it, Ricci won't do it, and this man that is a tornado of hotness won't—even though a tiny part of me wants what he lays down at my feet.

Lariat scowls. "It doesn't have to be for real." He puts my messy hair behind my ear and wraps his long fingers around my bare neck. The gesture about undoes me.

Almost. I teeter on the brink of a *yes*.

Then I listen to his words replay in my mind. His bid for me to be his "old lady" is a false one. He can't even vouch for me for real.

Whatever.

I ignore the sucking chest wound that seeps blood and guts between us and do what must be done.

Slapping my cool lawyer face on, I nod, step away, and duck underneath his arm, scooping my purse and gun from the ground as I do.

I retreat a few steps. "I'm sorry about Mini. God knows I take it as a personal failure on my part."

He frowns, studying me.

"But I'm nobody's property." I search out the other three guys who are with him, leaning casually against big bikes like his.

Their faces are hard, giving nothing away.

My attention returns to Lariat. "Thanks, but no thanks."

Lariat's huge hands fist into meat mallets, the same hands that left tracks of fire all over my body.

And on my heart, I belatedly realize.

I swallow, sensing what I might be giving up.

In the end, I'm protecting him. But Lariat doesn't need to know that.

Ever.

"Angel, don't be stupid. You can't fight the mafia. It doesn't work."

He knows they were here, threatening me. Somehow, Lariat knows.

I glance at him, my hand on the door handle. He steps back and I open the car door and slide inside. I insert the key blindly through a wash of tears and turn the engine over. Pressing the button, the window rolls down.

We stare at each other for a heartbeat then Lariat closes the small distance to my car, his hands gripping the top of the window frame where the glass is halfway open.

"Don't do this."

His face is hard and unsettled when I turn and look at him. A streetlamp inside the cemetery perfectly illuminates us both.

"I'm not stupid, and I *am* doing this. Goodbye, Lariat."

I press the window button again and the glass ascends, establishing a barrier between us.

He steps back, big hands dropping to his sides.

Reversing, I turn the car around and force my eyes off the rearview mirror.

I can't watch through my wave of fresh tears as Lariat becomes a receding dot in the reflection.

14

LARIAT

Fuck *her*.

Fuck Angel twice. Oh yeah, I already did.

I stalk back over to the guys, swing a leg over my seat, plant my ass on the bike, and shelve hard fists against my thighs.

"How'd that go?" Noose asks to the sky, cig jammed in his craw. Perfect loops of smoke rise to be eaten by the dark.

"Why don't you shut the fuck up and give me a smoke?" I answer without missing a beat.

Noose cracks a smile and jerks his chin up. "Testy."

Leaning forward, my middle finger pops out of my fist.

"Hey now, Lariat, that's Noose's trademark, not yours," Wring comments.

I grunt, my mood so foul I can't think past it. I know those mob dicks were around. I saw the depressions in the grass from footprints. And I saw Angel's heartbeat thumping in her throat from residual fear.

I also see the remnants of a bullet hole in the perfection of the graveyard lawn.

My eyes follow Snare as he moves like liquid to the spot I just noticed. Stooping, he takes something from the ground. He's doing what I should've been doing, but I'm too fucking unnerved to explore shit. Angel's aloof face keeps riding in the forward edge of my brain.

He lifts something small between his fingers. "Slug just lying around in the cemetery—nice."

"Gun fired," Wring states, narrowing his eyes at Snare, who nods.

"I'd say—not that I'm one of those forensic dicks." He winks. "But looks like it was your girl who did the shooting."

I nod. "Yup." I saw her pick up the gun and her purse.

"She blow you off?" Noose asks with a flick of inch-long ash.

"Yup." My gut rebels, doing a slow, thick leap and roll. "Fuck her."

"Just restating the obvious," Snare begins in a dry voice, "but sounds like you did that, brother."

Hate him voicing my earlier thoughts. Because they're true.

"Just pussy," Wring says, crossing his arms and lifting his chin, giving me a dead stare. "That's all she has to be. You didn't petition Viper with old lady status."

"And the tie is broken," Noose states in a low voice. "Mini is gone, man. You don't owe this bitch."

I nod again. I'm doing a lot of that lately. "I know. More than that, I want to know who killed Mini in prison. *Why*." My gaze scores them with my contained grief. "Mini was in there because she murdered a man who was beating her. Okay. Sure, she could have done it in self-defense instead of bashing his brains in while he slept."

Chuckles all around.

"But she didn't. Why would anyone else give a shit about your cousin but you, Lariat?" Snare's words are hard, but his eyes hold compassion.

The silence is complete.

Noose shrugs. "Maybe it has nothing to do with Mini."

My eyes slim on him. "What do ya mean?" The whole fucking convo is painful as fuck. Mini was all the family I had left.

Now I have nothing, not even Angel. But I never had her, not really.

"I'm saying," Snare says slowly, "maybe Mini was killed because of the lawyer."

"Angel?" I make a noise somewhere between a cough and a grunt. "No way."

Snare rolls his shoulders, striding back. He opens his palm, and a shell casing from a small gun gleams dully in the pale light from the streetlamp inside the cemetery.

"She had company." Noose's pale gray eyes look eerily silver with the artificial pool of bluish illumination cast by the streetlamp.

"Yeah, she did."

"She knows we're former SEALs. Like we wouldn't know when a weapon's been discharged."

A laugh shoots outta me. "I think Angel suspects we know. And what I find truly fucking fascinating is she didn't ask how we all showed up, Johnnies-on-the-spot-style."

"She's running scared," Wring says factually. "Reacting. Not thinking shit through."

I cock my head and slant a look his way. "What do you mean?"

"Really?" Wring leans back and folds his arms over his muscular chest. He has been seriously hitting the weights, and it shows. "What I think is she's into you, but Angel doesn't know how to handle it. What with her client getting killed and the mob up her ass. Then you charge in there without a plan and start popping other lawyers in the face."

I lace my fingers together, noting that Noose didn't hand over a cig yet. "Sounds plausible when you line it out like that," I finally say.

"Trying to think like a chick is exhausting, but I'm married to one now. And some of their chaotic thought process makes a sort of dim sense."

I laugh, my eyebrow quirking. "So it's not all about pussy, eh?"

Wring shakes his head. "Shannon was so sheltered and innocent, I felt guilty for getting a hard-on."

Noose barks out a laugh. "You got over that pronto, though."

Wring rubs a hand over his short flattop. His full wasp coloring glows under the light. "Yeah. So over it."

"Men—we just fight it out, and shit gets resolved," Noose says.

Well…yeah. And the point is?

"But chicks, they get all buried in their emotions and don't figure shit out. Even someone as smart as Angela Monroe might not see the forest for the trees. Ya get me?" Noose's eyebrows rise.

I do and yank a shoulder up. "But she still told me to fuck off."

"She did? In those words?" The corners of Wring's lips twitch.

I glare. "No, asshole, in *Angel* words."

"Which were?" Snare asks.

Confession time. "I asked her to be my property." My voice is so low, the guys lean forward to catch my words.

Noose whistles low in his throat, and I ignore him, continuing. "Then when she didn't seem on board, I told her it could just be for looks, that the status would protect her."

Noose flicks his spent cig on the ground, and a small spark smolders like a dying firefly. "Mob's still going to romance her. Or whatever the blue fuck they're doing."

"See, that's it—I don't know *what* they're up to. But that limp fuck Tommy was sent to beat her down." I spread my arms away from my body. "I stopped that."

Wring, Noose, and Snare remain silent.

"Then they obviously put the moves on her today, but I didn't see any new damage on Angel. Thank fuck."

"We'd have to pop some melons for that shit." Noose gives a small salute, commenting as though he's talking about the weather instead of bringing death.

The brothers nod. We don't fuck around when we're committed. We do what needs to be done.

"So let's go over the bullshit," Wring says, ticking off points on his fingers. "Angel is being pursued by—what's that fucker's name?"

"Antonio Ricci," Noose interjects because he knows all that intel shit already, I'd speculate.

Wring snaps his fingers sharply. "While he's in the pen. And your cousin—sorry to say, Lariat—gets killed right after Angel gets mauled by a mob prick. Not liking the coincidence."

"Yeah."

"Right after you save her and get biblically acquainted."

I scowl at Wring.

"Not asking for deets, my brother, just laying out the facts as they appear from the outside lookin in."

"Fine." I spin my hand like *Get talking.*

"Where'd you put the GPS locator, since you mentioned her transport is trashed?"

I smile like a shark.

Noose sits up from his slouch on the bike seat straight as an arrow. "Like that grin, have to say."

"On the gun."

"No shit?" Noose laughs. "Fucking pure, man. Nice."

"You figured Angel was paranoid about her situation?" Wring asks.

I tilt my head. "Absolutely. It's as though I show up, go caveman on her, and Angel acts as if she's still on her own with nobody having her back."

Snare frowns. "You heard what that mouthpiece Al said. She's had a rough background."

I turn from Snare to Noose.

We maintain serious eye contact, and he snatches my question out of thin air. "I can do it, man, but don't kill the messenger. I found out serious shit on Shannon, and Wring was *not* a fan." Noose holds up a palm then slaps it on his thigh.

Wring scowls at him, brows dipping low.

"I need to know what kind of woman I'm working with," I say.

Noose snorts, lighting another cigarette. "I didn't give a fuck what Rose was before me. It was all about what she was with me, brother. Think about that. Maybe better ya don't know. Just let shit happen instead of planning it all to fucking death." He lifts a shoulder, blowing out two smoke rings that are almost stacked they're so tight.

"I want Mini's killer."

They look at me. And whatever shit that's still between Noose and me is there too. But at the end of the day, we fought together, got tortured together, ate together, and banged chicks together. Hell, we're *tighter* than brothers. I can say anything. I can say what I want, and they wouldn't laugh or condemn me.

It's still fucking hard, though. "And"—I tear a palm over my face, scrubbing it back and forth and noticing I need a shave—"I want Angel protected."

Wring grins. "You just want Angel. Period. Don't bullshit us, Lariat. You might be the quietest one. And fuck knows, you're not into sentiment."

I quirk a brow at him.

Noose laughs. "No shit." His grin fades. "But if we're going to run all over hell's half-acre, shadowing this woman, give us a *reason* to."

"With actual fucking words," Snare adds.

I talk to my hands. "Angel doesn't want me."

"Like that matters how?" Noose asks.

I don't force chicks. Hell, I would never beg. What the fuck is so different about this one?

"We can't help who we want," Wring states with a shrug.

"Okay," I announce, turning on my engine. "I'm done with the circle jerk. I just wanna make sure Angel's okay. Whether she wants it or not."

Snare straddles his seat, threading his hands together and placing them on his head. He pumps his hips. "See"—*thrust, swivel*—"if she's okaaaaay." He tilts his hips and does an obscene fast pump, hands behind his head as if he's a posing porn star.

"Fuck off," I say. "And when you're done fucking off here, fuck off to the end of the street. And when you're done fucking off there, fuck off to...I don't know—*California*."

Snare doesn't hear me though because the brothers are too busy laughing.

"All you fuckers." I dismiss them with a wave, revving my motor over their guffawing bullshit.

Noose recovers first. "I'll open Pandora's box. But don't get pissed with what I find."

I relax against my seat for a second. "Fine."

We exchange nods.

Noose turns on his ride, pulls smoothly away, and the rest of us follow.

Snare's got a twinkle in his eye as if he has a death wish.

But I don't give him much mind. My thoughts are on Angel and her rejection.

I won't beg.

However, I'm not above some first-rate convincing.

15

ANGEL

"Holy shit, Ang," Trudie says, swiping a thick lock of chestnut hair behind her shoulder. "I don't hear from you for a week, and all this shit happens? *Pfft.*"

Trudie's my friend. But more than that, we shared the last foster home together. Not the one where I was molested and beaten for two years, but the next one. The one with a family not too dissimilar from my bio-family that died.

Trudie knows the entire truth. She's the only person alive who does. But when someone knows a person's history, she becomes pretty insightful, like now.

"So this biker guy—Lariat?"

I nod.

"He beats the shit out of Tommy, the mob bozo who's been skulking around, then he gets you home safe and sound." Her full lips lift at the corners. "Then you proceed to use every surface to sex him up."

"Yeah." I look at my hands, not in embarrassment, but because I feel stupid, even though my pussy gives a pleasant throb at the mention of multi-surface sex. "It wasn't my best decision."

"I thought you're a love em and leave em."

I lift my chin, and our eyes meet. Hers are a true, clear, root-beer brown.

I jerk my shoulder up quickly then let it drop. "Exactly."

"I've only heard about guys when they gave you multiple orgasms. It wasn't about the love, Ang."

Never about love. "I don't love Lariat, Trudie." I can barely keep the disdain out of my voice.

"Uh-huh." She's clearly unconvinced.

I frown. "I met him less than a week ago. No chance to even get to know a person in that span of time."

Trudie folds her windshield-wiper arms. "I'd say you know him better than most men, Ang. I mean, for you, you're practically dating."

I tense. "I don't date."

She nods slowly, searching my face, and I look away, unable to maintain eye contact.

"I understand that. Believe me, I know better than anyone why."

I cross my arms and am smart enough to recognize my defensive posture.

Trudie's silence is deafening.

She stands suddenly, leaving me to stew, and strolls to her small kitchen.

A shockingly crimson tea kettle is whistling, and she removes it from the burner then pours scalding water over Good Earth tea bags. I'm a coffee girl myself, but Trudie won't have it. Her house, her rules.

If she smothers the tea with honey, I can choke the brew down. She does, hiking the plastic bear high and squeezing an obscene amount of golden goo inside the cup. The spoon makes beautiful clinking sounds as she stirs the mix.

Trudie walks back, and I admire how self-contained she is. She knows who she is, and after obtaining an English degree, she has decided to become a medical transcriptionist. In her own words, she doesn't want to be office-bound. She wants to have a nomadic lifestyle and see the world. Have Wi-Fi, will travel.

I look around her apartment, which is decorated in Pier One chic. I love it, though it's not my thing. Trudie's colorful and casual personality shows through every pillow and throw rug, even the teacups we drink from. Seashells and sea glass from her travels are piled haphazardly inside a shallow, antique basket on the center of her low-slung coffee table.

Trudie is just renting this small apartment. She'll be traveling for good when her one-year medical transcription course is satisfied.

I'll miss her so much. The thought of Trudie leaving makes my chest feel as if a stone of despair is lodged in its center.

As if reading my thoughts, she says, "Take a sabbatical. You don't have much of a life, anyway."

I snort, rolling my eyes, but her words stop my self-pity. "Gee, thanks, Trudie."

She's right.

"I'm right, and you know it," she says, echoing my thoughts. "Come with me." She grabs my hand. "Get lost in life. Stop trying to force living—just *be*."

I turn her hand over in mine and trace the lifelines on her palm.

"I can't. I told you about Mini Dreyfus."

Our hands release, and she sighs. "I can't believe the coincidence of this mess. You go to the only living relative your client has and manage to secure bail. Then he randomly saves you from a mob dickhead."

The whole series of events does have a surreal flavor.

"*Then*," she chortles, "you do him—*everywhere*."

I actually blush at this point.

"See." Trudie points at me. "You can't believe it, either."

I give a soft shake of my head. "I can't, but my God, he was magnificent. Is."

"You care about him," she presses, studying my face.

I nod helplessly. "I don't *want* to. But he's the first man, besides my dad, who's ever stood up for me."

Trudie covers my hand with her own. "Ang, there are men out there who don't hurt women. They're all over the place."

"I can't tell who is who," I whisper.

A tear slides down my face and hangs like a tremulous wet diamond. It lands on Trudie's hand.

"This guy, this biker dude—he's for real. If he was going to hurt you, he could have. Hell, he stomped Tommy."

Accurate.

"And he made you feel safe enough that you broke your one-fuck rule."

My smile slides into place, and I laugh. "So true." I flatten my palms on my flaming cheeks.

"Begin with him. Use him if you have to."

My eyes meet hers. "It's not possible to use a guy."

Trudie leans back in her overstuffed chair, which is a rich, deep royal purple. "They're human beings too, you know. Men. Just because a guy has a penis doesn't mean he doesn't feel things."

"They're all about the pussy, Trudie."

"Not all of them. They like what we have, sure. But eventually, everyone wants more—more contact, companionship, you name it. It's the human state of being."

I bite my lip. "Maybe."

"You know what's really bugging me?" Trudie asks, leaning forward.

I shake my head, dead certain she'll share, and just that thought makes me grin.

My smile is stolen with her words. "I hate this mob deal that's happening. How long has it been since you put that criminal behind bars?"

My exhale sounds exhausted, even to my own ears. "Two years. I was fresh out of law school." I lean back, suddenly wiped. "I was so green, ready to make a name for myself. Clean up the system, justice be served, and all that propaganda."

Trudie nods, her hands dangling between skinny legs. Her dark rich brown hair falls forward as she plucks her cup off the dainty saucer. She takes a sip and sets it down again.

"So Ricci kills the witness in this gruesome way."

I shudder, giving a curt nod.

"I'm sorry. I know it's got to be hard to talk about."

My silence is answer enough.

"But…" Trudie hesitates as if articulating whatever she's about to say will make it real. Words have power. We both know that. "Why beat you up? Then say that the godfather guy wants to bring you on board?" Her brows push together. "There's no way you'd do that, Ang." Her eyes roam my face. "I know that. They've *got* to. I mean, you're responsible for putting him away." She rolls her bottom lip between her teeth. "Then there's that cryptic comment about your dad."

Our gazes lock.

"Yeah," I say softly, positive my uncertainty leaks through my expression.

"Do you think there's anything to it?"

My heart screams *no*, but my intellect casts doubt. "Why would he say that unless there was some part that was true?"

"But your dad was chill."

I nod. "Best dad ever. I had a great childhood before..."

Arnold Jenkins, we both think but don't say.

"There's something in all this that links these things together. You're clearly at the center. And I'm not going to lie, I'm scared to pieces for you."

My palms dampen at her words, and I fist my fear with my hands. "I fought them off."

Trudie shakes her head. "You took them by surprise, *and* they don't want you dead. They didn't have guns, right?"

"No guns."

She pauses for a beat. "Tommy didn't work you over this time?"

"No." My lips twitch. "Didn't give him a chance."

Trudie's return smile is wan as she plants her elbows on her knees and props her face up. "I'm stumped, then."

I unclench my jaw. "They won't stop."

Trudie's eyes meet mine. "No way, they're after you." Her face brightens. "Duh." She slaps her thigh. "Get the police involved."

"Shit, the police are *already* involved." I proceed to tell her about Brad.

Trudie's sigh is irritated. "Brad just wants to get into your panties. He's in the middle of finding out about a client's death, but he takes time out to grill you about Lariat." She gives a hard eye roll. "Douche."

My eyes flip to the ceiling for a long moment.

"Don't roll those pretty topaz eyes at me, Angela Monroe."

"I can't help it." I slap my hands on the couch. "Who cares about Brad at a time like this?"

Her exhale is pure disbelief. "Because Brad's a turd—a smart one. He's going to try and make trouble for this Lariat guy, who's ex-Navy SEAL, right?"

I bite my bottom lip. "Yes, more assassin than anything." Another angle to worry about.

Trudie's light-brown eyebrows pull together. "That's not true at all. I had a cousin who was in. Patriotic group. They're tight, and they follow orders, go where nobody else will. They saved that young gal a few years ago. Remember?"

I kind of do, it was covered heavily in the media. A girl about nineteen, if I remember right. "But no other survivors?"

Trudie leans forward. "What I'm saying is they're the best men. They are vetted to fucking death, Ang. If this Lariat guy's been a SEAL, he didn't give up their code just because he separated form the Navy. He's honorable."

I don't say anything. Lariat has been crude—rough around the edges doesn't even cover it. He has also been protective and smart.

Mouthwatering. I can't forget how he felt moving deep inside of me.

I press a hand to my stomach, trying to quiet butterflies that won't be shut down just because I will it. The intense sex we shared won't go away. Those memories aren't a stain like the ones I bore when I was harmed as a child. They're fresh, good memories, covering the ones I have such a hard time shaking.

"I told him I didn't want to be his old lady—property—whatever the hell that means." I don't want to be owned by anyone.

I squeeze my eyes shut at the image flashing inside my mind of him owning my body.

I had loved that.

"Oh, Ang, he wasn't trying to dominate your ass."

My eyes swing to her. "You can't imagine what he was like, what he did to Tommy, so quickly, so smooth… casual. As though it was no effort."

"Like us?" she asks. And I know she is referring to all the hours of self-defense classes we mastered together.

I snort. "He makes us look like amateurs. For one thing, like I think I mentioned no less than twice, he's six feet four if he's an inch."

"That's one tall mofo."

"Uh-huh."

"Must be weird for you," Trudie the pixie elf says.

I smirk. "It *is* weird. But great," I admit quietly. "I feel so sheltered. Protected."

"Owned?" Her smile matches mine, knowing and happy.

"Yeah," I say in soft reflection. "He *was* pretty great."

"That doesn't have to be past tense."

I shake my head as if my thoughts are on fire. "Nope. I can't drag him into the middle of this. He has a chance to fly under the mob radar if I break off contact right now. I can't believe I'm even concerning myself over this budding romance when the mob is breathing down my neck. Shows where my small Pooh-brain is at."

Trudie's face screws up into a frown, but she chuckles. I notice she doesn't deny my small-brain status. "I'm just wondering…how did Lariat and his fellow bikers happen to just show up exactly when things were getting scary with Tommy and crew?"

I scrunch my nose, thinking. "I'm not sure. Another fact to get scared over."

"But the mob scares you worse."

I nod. "They found me practically at my parents grave."

"I bet they're GPS-ing your ass. Do you have a locator turned on with your cell?"

"No." I shrug. "Got wrecked with the Tommy thing. I'm currently phoneless. Except." I hold up my burner phone.

Trudie chews a thumbnail, giving a distracted nod. "I think I'd want to die without a cell and all its smart thoughts. So *I* don't have to think, uh-huh." She's silent for a few seconds. "I want answers."

"You and me both."

She pops off the couch and walks into the small kitchen then opens the fridge and rummages around. She slides out a small glass dish and pops the entire thing in the microwave.

My mouth waters. "Please tell me that is some awesome leftovers."

Trudie nods happily. A hobbyist cook, she loves to fix food, but she says it's better to cook for more than just one. Usually, it's as though she's cooking for ten. Trudie always cooks too much. As skinny as she is, I would think she would want to gorge on her own cooking, but she doesn't. She has spent too many years going without.

I got raped and beaten, and Trudie got starved.

What a pair we make.

We thought we'd won the lottery when we were placed with the Phillips.

So she obsessively cooks and is still as thin as a rail, and I don't date men. I just fuck them. Once.

Except Lariat.

It doesn't take more visits to a psychiatrist to understand that my one-fuck rule is mainly about control. Because I finally can control things.

Trudie walks over. Her hand is encased in an oven mitt, and her fingers are wrapped around the steaming food. She sets the dish down before me on the coffee table, lifts the lid, and lays a fork beside it.

Lasagna covered in homemade sauce with chunks of tender ground beef releases lazy spirals of vapor that swirl from the dish.

"Wait!" she announces and runs to the cupboard, where she snags a stemmed crystal wine glass.

Yum. Wine and lasagna, Heaven on Earth.

"You are a good, good friend," I state as fact.

She saunters back with a pour that's more vat than glass. "I'm your only friend."

Trudie has her own glass, and we clink. "Touché."

We take long sips, our eyes meeting over the rims. She collapses against the soft chair. "Friends are like treasure. We're rich, you know."

I have a piece of lasagna dangling off my fork, but I don't take a bite. Tears swell my eyes again, and the view of Trudie is suddenly obscured.

"Don't cry, Ang," Trudie says in a breathy voice as her own eyes hold a shine. "Because then I'll have to. And I've wasted enough tears on the past."

I swallow my memories and agony down.

I have this moment—Trudie, good food, and wine. I must be brave. Getting to the bottom of this mess will take time.

"Why aren't you eating?" I ask between bites, juggling the too-hot spots.

Trudie shrugs. "Eating's for chumps."

"You're too thin."

Her look is sharp. "And you're scared of dating men."

Suddenly, my fine meal is not as satisfying, and I push the colorful dish away with a quarter of the food remaining. I set the clear glass lid on top, and it instantly fogs.

"I'm sorry," Trudie says, noticing my diminished appetite.

"It's a struggle."

Our gazes lock. "For both of us," she admits.

I nod. "We do the best we can. I don't like to see you go hungry, though."

"And I don't like to see you deny yourself a chance at happiness."

I reach for Trudie at the same time she reaches for me. We stand, coming together in an over-the-coffee-table hug. She's so petite that she practically disappears in my arms.

Trudie squeezes me tightly, despite her size. "I love you, sister."

"I love you more," I say and mean every word.

A knock sounds at the door, and we pull back from each other. I look at her questioningly.

"Don't know." She unwraps herself from me and moves toward the door.

I have a sudden thought of the mafia and gracelessly stumble out of the tight confines between the couch and table. But Trudie is already opening the door.

Lariat fills the space.

His eyes meet mine, and it might have gone differently if he'd just been calm.

But Lariat is not hardwired that way. He bangs open the door and moves to enter Trudie's place.

"No!" I scream, anticipating Trudie.

And Trudie doesn't hesitate. My partner in self-defense… defends.

And things go from bad to worse.

16

LARIAT

Just because I stopped being a SEAL doesn't mean my heart doesn't stay one.

I claim that man forever—the one who fought for his country and bleeds for it after my duty was done.

The bike rumbles between my thighs in warm comfort as I follow the tracking attached to Angel's weapon.

That state-of-the-art techie shit is courtesy of Noose from a while ago. Never used one of those before and didn't think I would need to. Until Angel.

Now I'm following her around like some pussy-whipped stalker. I've been dismissed and handed my walking papers. Angel has made it clear she won't even *pretend* to be my property to save her own skin.

It seems as though she has been doing her own defending for a long time.

I pull up in front of a 1990s ritzy apartment complex that looks dated but well-maintained. It has the unfortunate luck of being on the east hill of Kent, where valley meets cresting hill. The development is adjacent to Valley Keys, an old subsidized collection of homes from the 1950s and 60s. Originally intended to help poor families, the complex now houses every immigrant living off our welfare system that it can pack in.

My lip lifts in disgust. Not because my ass is so lily white and perfect. But because I defended every person who lives in our country, even those who will never know the sacrifice or appreciate it.

They sleep, while I don't. They listen to sudden, loud noises and don't feel as if their gut just became one with the ground.

Maybe their brains process fucking sharper because they don't have the muddled and sometimes incoherent shit I sort through day by day. But I was *me* for hours while I was with Angel. She brought me back to whatever fucked-up center I owned before the sandbox. She gave me the gift of clarity for a few hours.

I want more than a taste of that, more than the brief appetizer we had at her place. I don't want the thought to form, but it does without my permission: Maybe I even want something more than sex.

That realization scares the fuck out of me—the want of more. But I've never been a coward. And I'm willing to fight for the chance, even if she gives me that bullshit line about how we're not going to work.

We worked so well, it shook the foundation of my world.

I climb suspended steps made of aggregate concrete, tiny pebbles and agates embedded in the treads, and hike the staircase toward where that signal takes me. The GPS device is slotted at the bottom of the sliding clip of her piece. It is designed to be integral but not interfere with discharge or be affected by heat.

Perfect and brilliant.

I move to the door that has pitted brass numerals. It reads 203.

Spreading my fingers on the wood door, I lean in and press my ear to the panel.

I close my eyes and slacken my jaw, hearing the modulation of feminine voices.

One in particular, I recognize, and my cock gives a confirming nod.

Nice.

I rap hard on the wood, and the voices stop. I step away and raise my hand, ready to pound on the door a second time.

The solid wood door swings wide, and a tiny chick clutches the edge. She has light-brown eyes and dark rich-brown hair, which is fairly long and circles her shoulders.

Needs a food funnel, skinny as fuck. I drop my assessment. My eyes travel the room, and I see Angel attempting to move between crammed furniture, coming toward the door on more or less of a race pace.

A grim smile plasters my face, and I flat-palm the door wider. With a smack of my palm, it bangs off the wall.

We're getting crap figured out, regardless of her little friend as audience or whatever bullshit story she's making herself believe.

We got something, something rare, and I want to explore it.

I want Angel. And like some pussy, I want her on almost any terms she'll have me.

Then there's an elbow in my gut—a precise, well-thought-out maneuver.

I was *not* expecting that shit. I double over and snap my hand out like a striking snake, grabbing onto a slim forearm by total instinct.

"No!" Angel shouts.

Not gonna hurt your friend, I have time to think. Then her knee hits my balls like a club to the face.

Nausea roars, and I reevaluate breathing.

I sink to my knees and haul her down to the floor with me. With the flat of my palm and what remaining oxygen I have wheezing through my nose, I hold the friend still, my palm to her chest.

She tries to take out my eyeballs with her thumbs around where I'm pressing her chest to the ground.

Fuck *me.*

"Trudie! Quit! It's Lariat."

Angel shoves me, and I fall on my ass in the most shameful display of getting my clock cleaned that I've ever had in my life. My dick feels like a swollen mass of agony.

Tough Navy SEAL, taken down by a one-hundred-pound female.

Jesus, what a nightmare.

"What?" she shrieks, and I think she has deafened me as well as trying to kill chances for future children.

"It's Lariat," Angel repeats, glaring at me, and my cock tries to work through its current anguish to respond.

Amazing.

I blink at her, still trying to speak. Finally, I manage with a rasping choke of words. "Coming by to check on you."

"Well, don't," she says. Half rant and half fear make her words like knives.

They slash and chop at my already wounded male pride. I look down at the friend.

She opens that pouty mouth. "You could've just said something like, hey, I'm Lariat, but *noooo*. You just he-man in the door and go after her. Kind of a stupe move, you know, being as how Angel's just told me the mafia is on her tail. Duh."

I blink again. "I'm not the mob, and holy Christ, you think you could just *not* attack someone just because they open the door?"

A smile tweaks her lips, and I start to smile too.

"Yeah, six foot *oh my God* of muscled caveman bursts through the door, and I just, I don't know, let him waltz in? Do you think I'm dumb?"

Insane broad. I shake my head. Dumb is a no-go.

She starts to laugh, and I join in then groan at the disaster of my junk. *Fucking kills.*

Before long, Angel is shaking her head. "You guys, God." Her voice is shaky, and she sinks to her heels, knees bent. "Trudie, he's right. What if it had been someone else?"

She doesn't say Tommy's name, but it's in the air between us.

"You didn't spend a lot of time on Lariat's looks," the friend comments slyly.

My eyebrow pops as my stomach finally begins to quiet. I might not spew chunks after all. I give Angel a questioning stare.

She's blushing so hard, her freckles look as though they'll burn off her skin.

"Trudie of the big mouth"—Angel sweeps her hand at Trudie—"this is Lariat."

"Of the big cock?" Her light-brown eyebrow arches, and a laugh bursts out of me.

"No shit?" I jerk Angel onto my lap and smooth her unruly hair away from her face, cupping her cheek in my hand. "You've been talking about my cock while the mob is after you?" I can't keep the laughter out of my voice.

"Trudie obviously didn't hit you hard enough," she grumbles, but nothing can take away my pleasure in knowing that with everything going on, she's still thinking about our time and the parts of me that gave her pleasure.

"She hit me hard enough." I slant a nasty glare Trudie's way. She would make other guys shake in their boots.

Trudie kicks her chin up and gives me the bird.

I'm quiet for a second, studying her defiant posture. "I think I like her," I comment slowly.

Angel's lips flatten as she clearly tries to contain her laughter. "Yeah, I'll keep her."

And just like that, the communication opens up. If only it would be about the shit I want to resolve.

☠

I stifle a groan as I shift my weight on the dainty couch, my nuts dully throbbing. I look the place over, noticing a shawl-type thing on the back of a purple chair. *Is that beaded fringe*? I shake my head.

Place is hippy hollow.

"So, let me get this straight," Trudie begins, and I plant my face in my hand.

"You've put a GPS chip on Angel's gun?"

I yawn. "Yeah."

"Am I boring you?"

I'm not much of a talker, more of a doer. I'm not getting dick for sleep either—running on fumes. "I want
to take Angel somewhere safe until this mob shit gets
handled. I'm looking into how Mini was killed. Got a
man on the inside. We'll know what's what in hours." I
lean back, biting the inside of my cheek against the pain.
Bitch nailed me.

I frown. I guess I'm still pissed at getting handled
by a chick because my guard was down. I looked at the
packaging and dismissed the girl.

Won't happen again.

I ask myself for the second time—where were both
girls taught self-defense?

I adjust my junk, and Trudie coughs out a laugh.
"You a confident man, Lariat?"

"No," I spit. "My dick hurts because you kneed me
in the nuts."

"God, he's choice, Ang. You know how to pick them."

"Who's saying I have?" Angel replies in a cool voice.

God. *Damn.*

My face swivels to her. "You're making me crazy. I
don't give two fucks and a shit if Trudie listens in. We
have something, whether you try to rationalize it or not.
I tried to offer you the easiest protection I could. You
refused." I make sure every bit of how stupid I think that
decision is bleeds into my tone.

By the pissed-off look washing her face, I hit the
mark dead-on.

"I think everything's linked, and I know those mob cocksuckers were at the graveyard. I want to know exactly what was said. If I'm informed, I can help. Not when I'm a mushroom and fed shit in the dark."

Trudie snorts, but Angel is behind that mask again— the one I figure she wears when she's not interested in doing emotion.

Great. We got that in common.

"I didn't get bail arranged fast enough. Mini's dead." Her voice catches, and she draws a shaky inhale.

"It's not your fault," Trudie and I say like clones.

Angel's smile is watery as her eyes move between us in clear denial. "Maybe, but it doesn't change that it happened."

I stand, towering over where Angel sits—as far away from me as she can get. As if she's scared what might happen with closer proximity.

I hunker down beside the glaring violet chair and wince as my balls shriek against the denim. "Listen, just humor me. Take a few days off."

"I have court," Angel says, refusing to look at me.

My eyes run over the barely-beginning-to-heal bruise on her face. "I don't care if the president's coming to visit." I curl a finger underneath her chin and force her to look deeply into my eyes. "I want you safe until we can figure out what the fuck is going on."

"Why?" she whispers. "Is this some kind of guilt thing because of Mini?"

I shake my head. "It has nothing to do with Mini." I pause for a second, reconsidering. "Everything."

Angel's pitch-black eyebrows pull together. "Which is it? I'm confused."

"I was more than happy to help Mini—to know that she was alive. But I'm not *responsible* for her. I never got the chance to be."

"And you're not responsible for me, either, Lariat." She pleads for understanding with her eyes, begging me to bow out, to let her go.

Instead, I place her hand against my heart, knowing the thing's trying to knock out of my chest.

The skin of her hand warms me through my cut.

"Tell that to me here," I say in quiet command.

Angel's eyes dip to where her hand lies above my racing heart. Then her gaze flies up to my face.

I've never felt braver or more vulnerable.

I watch her expression crumble, warring with the need to stay distanced, to not believe that anyone could ever actually give a shit.

I lift her from the chair and set her on my lap.

"I can't believe you," she whispers against my skin.

"You don't need to," I reply quietly, my lips on her throat. "I believe enough for both of us."

Trudie's loud voice shatters the moment. "If you break it off with this stud, I'm going to personally take time out to kick your ass too, Ang."

Angel's fingers crawl up my chest, and her arms gradually encircle my neck. She lays her cheek on my chest.

"I can't fight you both, I suppose," she admits, and I hear the smile in her voice.

I shake my head. "Don't try."

Trudie laughs. "I like him."

"Me too," Angel whispers, too low for her friend to hear but loud enough for me to have hope.

17

ANGEL

"*That's* how you keep finding me?" I drag out my gun and give it a thorough inspection, but I can't find the GPS microchip.

Lariat smirks. "Figured you were paranoid enough after Tommy's bullshit that you'd hang onto the piece."

I slide my gun back home inside my handbag and sigh. The exhale feels dragged out of me. "Yes, you were right."

"Hey, stud."

Lariat turns to Trudie.

She snorts, folding her slim arms. "Like the way you take orders."

He glowers.

I snicker.

"Can't win with you two broads."

"Broad, huh?" Trudie steps forward, and Lariat retreats a half step.

"Scared?" she asks.

A smile ghosts his lips. "Cautious. You got a set of balls on ya, and I'm not hurting a woman."

"Hmmm." Trudie taps her angular jaw with a nail. "I think Ang is good here for the moment. You can take all your leather and"—she waves her hand around—"testosterone overload out of here. Get back with us when you find out about her client." Trudie's light-amber eyes softly glow as she pauses before speaking in a more sub-dued tone. "Your cousin."

We're all silent at that, and I struggle not to cry again. Seems as though I've been drowning in a river of my own grief lately.

I haven't had a moment's pause to think straight.

Lariat puts his hands on his hips, staring Trudie down. "I agree with the part that Angel is safe here—for the moment. But the mafia's not going away." His stare lands on me for a moment then returns to Trudie. "We won't know what we're dealing with until we find out why my cousin was murdered inside the prison."

"I don't think Angel's client's murder is related to the current catastrophe of the mafia."

I shake my head. "Tommy was busy nursing his wounds on the ground, but one of the flunkies said my dad was involved with Ricci."

"That's bullshit. You've told me everything you could remember about your folks. Daddy was a golden boy. Your mom was Martha Stewart."

My laugh is harsh as I shrug. "Yes, they were."

"Go to the police. Make a spectacle," Trudie pleads.

"No," Lariat and I say together then exchange an uneasy glance.

"You go first," I tell him, wondering what his reasoning is.

He drags a large palm over his face, and I notice the darkened skin underneath eyes as black as pitch. "Don't know what boy in blue we can trust. Who might be on the payroll."

"Why do you figure that?" Trudie asks innocently.

Lariat's lips twist sarcastically. "Call it a hunch."

Plenty of MC people pay off cops, I speculate.

Lariat's inky eyebrows rise, and he snorts out a laugh. "I'm not real popular around there right now."

"Because you punched Brad," I state dryly.

Trudie's eyes go wide. "He did?"

I nod.

"Love *that*. Brad is always such a condescending nubby dick. Loves himself. Probably breaks his neck passing by mirrors."

"Nubby dick?" Lariat's laugh is abrupt. "I got the feeling he's his own groupie." He frowns. "I thought Brad was doing something to Angel."

"He wasn't. Brad's just worried about me," I admit, not tacking on the *because I'm with you* part. I neither confirmed or denied that with Brad.

"Brad's a sleaze in a suit," Lariat states, and I'm ticked he makes his character out so fast.

"We do the same job. Brad's smart." I don't know why I'm defending him. I've said no every time he wanted to take me out. I agree with Lariat. Brad's sort of sleazy, just a vibe I get off him. Though I've never sought to confirm my instincts, or had any definitive proof.

But I screwed Lariat against the wall within hours of knowing him—not a rousing endorsement of my morals. I feel heat rise with regard to my casting of stones. I would be the first one on the list.

I can tell by his expression that Lariat misinterprets my blush.

"Are you fucking gone on him?" Lariat asks.

"No," I rush to answer then reply more calmly. Though it's none of his business, I feel compelled to elaborate. "I don't date people I work with."

"Thank God for small favors," Trudie mutters.

"Not for him not wanting you, right?" Lariat asks with clear menace.

"You know, there were guys before this *thing*." I move my finger between us.

Lariat strides to me and and wraps me against him.

I can't breathe or think with him this near. The flush returns, but for entirely different reasons.

"God, that's *hot*," Trudie remarks in a hushed voice.

It's easy to forget Trudie's there, that there's any audience at all.

Lariat's lips are on mine, teasing, coaxing my soul out in the open.

Helpless not to respond, I wrap my arms around his neck. He lifts me by my ass, and I twist my legs around his waist.

We break away to breathe, my fingers wrapped around his thick neck as he loosely holds my butt cheeks. Our stare could melt paint.

"Is *this* a thing?" Lariat asks quietly, his eyes looking so deeply inside my own, I feel naked, though he's seen every inch of me nude.

My swallow is a painful, dry click. *It is so a thing.* It's a thing that terrifies me while making me feel as if I'll die without it.

Without him.

Like the sun on the Earth, the rain that falls from the heavens—I'm fertile ground for Lariat, and I'll starve without him near me.

"Like I said," Trudie says slowly, "I'm thinking you need to see this *thing* through." She giggles. "Whatever this thing is."

"Trudie's no dummy," Lariat comments, laughter in his voice.

They're conspiring against me.

He lets me slide down the front of him and doesn't wince.

"You recover fast, stallion," Trudie says.

Lariat smirks. "With her around"—his dark eyes seek me like the sun behind a cloud—"there's no choice."

"Panty dropping doesn't even *begin* to cover Lariat," Trudie says, collapsing into the royal purple chair. She spreads her knees and mock fans her crotch. "Holy crows, I think I creamed my panties just *watching* him go after you."

With trembling fingers, I shove my hair back behind my ear. "The doing is—wow—just wow."

She screws her brows into a first-class frown. "I don't know what you're afraid of, Ang. I'd let that man consume me until there was nothing left. Lariat is a walking, talking, sex-on-a-lollipop. Lick him down, lady." Trudie leans forward, shaking her hand as if she's trying to calm down.

I know exactly how she feels. Trudie just got the peripheral wave of sexual yumminess. I was in the blazing heat of it.

She falls back again, and we're silent. "So, I hate to be a wet blanket on the chaos and drama that is your life, but I have to study for this huge final exam, when all I really want to do is figure out your mess."

Me too. "Lariat's gone off to"—I whip my palm back and forth—"find out information in probably the most illegal way possible." I dunk my face in my hands again. "I just don't want to know."

"Probably best," Trudie says in a droll voice.

"But maybe, for the first time in my life, I don't care. Or I'm trying not to think about it too much."

Trudie frowns. "Because you dig him or because your life is in danger?"

All of it. "All that." I stand. "Can I take a shower?"

"Mi casa es su casa." Trudie swings her palm toward where I know the bathroom is.

"Thank you," I say gratefully. "Do I still have some spare clothes sitting around?"

"I've got a drawer for you."

The edges of my lips tweak. "A drawer? An entire drawer?"

She nods happily. "Of course."

We walk into her tiny spare bedroom, and I rifle through said drawer, pulling out black yoga pants, underwear, and a thinnish lime-green T-shirt. "Perfect." I nod my appreciation at the comfort clothes.

Trudie jerks a thumb behind her. "Now that all that drama is over, I'm going to go plow through some studying."

"Hey," I say softly.

She turns, and the ends of her hair turn up, feathering just past her shoulders.

I take Trudie in my arms, folding her much smaller body against mine. "I love you."

Trudie hugs me back, hard. "I love you too."

I take a shower that is obscenely long, washing away what feels like ten days of grime instead of ten hours.

I winced away all the bruises and scrapes from the initial encounter with Tommy and washed my female bits twice.

A dissatisfied grunt threads through me that I couldn't finish what Lariat and I so obviously wanted to.

My face still hurts from being bashed, but I feel so much cleaner. Renewed.

I'm a little less scared of what's between Lariat and me. Of course, once that fear has been subdued, there's the real threat of Antonio Ricci to take its place. His long reach is clearly extending past his prison cell.

I don't think I can stand sitting here in Trudie's apartment until Lariat comes back to tell me what *really* happened to Mini.

When he left Trudie's apartment, I could tell how much he didn't want to go.

I could tell by the hand that cupped my face to the thumb that stroked over the wound Tommy put there. But I understood.

Lariat can't get the information he wants and stand bodyguard over me at the same time.

The thing is, that's Lariat's expectation for himself regarding a woman he's barely known inside of a weekend.

It's not *my* expectation of him. I don't have expectations of men. Actually, I do—bad ones.

Lariat has broken me of that part, at least where he's concerned. I should feel more concerned that he GPS'd my gun, but somehow, his watch care is a tally mark on the right side instead of the wrong.

I glance at my prepaid cell and press my thumb on the dock to check the time. It's late, nearly seven. I might have just enough time to go into the office and make peace with Brad. Plus, I need to explain my issues to Maryanne, who tried to help me—if I can catch them before they go home for the night.

The partners won't understand my involvement with Lariat. It won't look good.

I roll my lip between my teeth, lightly gnawing. *Do I care?*

I ruminate on the justice I've meted on others behalf—those who had no money to fight their own battles.

My memories of my father are like fingerprints of weight on my mind. Each fingertip that touches my brain reminds me of what he couldn't accomplish because of his death—his untimely death—and the resulting horror my life turned into because of his abbreviated life.

A fortifying inhalation later, I ask Trudie if I can take her car, it'll be safer than using the rental everyone can identify me in.

She moves her earphones to the side of her head, listening with one ear and pausing the practice exam on her laptop.

"Don't think that's a great plan, Ang." Her whiskey-colored eyes lay worry on me. "I mean, Lariat says he'll get answers in hours. He didn't like the idea of you leaving. I hate to say it, but I agree with him. "

"I have damage control to figure out. *If* I have a job. Jugtner, Cognate, and Anderson lost a client—violently."

I lost a client.

"And Brad got clocked. I left in the middle of drama, the likes of which have probably never darkened the doorstep of the firm."

Trudie swirls in her desk chair to face me, kicking her petite legs out in front of her and crossing them at the ankle. "Brad's a dick," she restates for the record.

I purse my lips. "Maybe, but he was worried, and Lariat punched him. I work with Brad. I owe him professional courtesy. I need to save my job." *If I can.* "I need for him *not* to press charges against Lariat."

"What do you think the partners are going to do if you come clean, Ang?"

I lift a shoulder.

"Tell them about this mob thing. Say you're being threatened, and this comes on top of Mini Dreyfus's death. What's wrong with being honest? You're more important than them saving face."

There's honest, and then there's *honest*. "They might be receptive, or they might distance themselves from what they see as a negative publicity liability. What if the media got a whiff of this? I wouldn't necessarily come off as a victim. I might be labeled as *involved* in a criminal capacity. Can you see that?" Not to mention, that with some careful sleuthing, my past might be dredged up again, without the protection of minor status.

I pace away in agitation. "Local lawyer sweetheart shames her dad's posthumous rep by getting a mob witness off, only to get him killed, and then gets approached by the same mafia." I make a sound of guttural disbelief deep in my throat. "Yeah, they'll have a field day with that one."

"You know, you're a goddamned negative Nancy. Why do you keep assigning these people's deaths to yourself? It makes no sense."

I don't know.

"You just want to suck up guilt to distract yourself from *living*. And I'm saying the words: you're *not* responsible for their deaths. You were involved in their *lives*. It could've been Brad working those cases."

My laugh is harsh. "He'd *never* do pro bono."

Trudie rolls her expressive eyes. "Okay, my point exactly. GQ is too busy grooming himself like an alley cat tonguing its fur instead of what he really should be tonguing."

My giggle bursts out of me. "Trudie…"

She cackles like a witch on crack. "Seriously? You're the only one in that place that steps in and does something for others. You take a hit on income to help people. Forget the guilt. It's not real or deserved. It's false guilt. Let Lariat the Stud help you." She wags her tongue then stands.

"God," I say, laughing. But my legs weaken with the memory of him between them.

Trudie laces her hands behind her head and swings her hips, making a parody of having a penis.

Her headphones slide off her head, clunking on the desk, but Trudie's not paying attention. She's *deep* in her role.

Grabbing her invisible appendage, she wags what looks like a fifteen-inch summer sausage around. "This is not Brad's, of course," she says with glee.

"Of course," I manage, but I'm doubled over, my ribs singing in agony.

"It's Lariat, right?" she howls.

I can't speak. Instead, I clutch at my ribs, praying to stop laughing.

Lariat doesn't have a foot-long penis.

I don't think.

18

LARIAT

"It gets worse," Noose says.

My chin nearly skims my chest, my head hanging low. *It can't get worse.*

"Angel was in that foster home for two years. With that sick fucker doing that shit to her."

I shake my head as though that'll get rid of the images that surface in response to Noose's information. "I can't stand to hear it."

"I'm sorry, man." Noose's clear gray eyes are dark with his rage. "There're some men that weren't in line when the man upstairs was passing out the hardware implant that men *protect* women."

"But she wasn't even a woman." I'm fucking sick to my toenails. My voice is a diseased thread between us.

Angela Monroe's parents died in a tragic car accident. There was no other family, so she got plugged into the system.

Okay.

But she didn't get placed with a good foster family. This one was bad. A full-grown man was raping and beating a kid. I've seen some horrors—lived them—but this is almost beyond my capacity to bear.

Angel bore it.

If she can survive that nightmare, I can listen to what happened.

"It's a fucking miracle Angel turned out the way she did. Smart, driven, helps other people. Hell, she's a poster child for overcoming."

I nod. "God, I wish I'd known. I wouldn't have—"

"Fuck that. You didn't treat her badly, man. She's almost twenty-seven years old. She makes choices now. Angela Monroe has had an ass-ton of therapy. I'm not saying she's well. I'm just saying she makes choices about her conduct and what she wants. Angel didn't have that luxury fifteen years ago; she has it now."

I suck in a lungful. "What else?" I let my breath out in a rush, bracing for more.

"Docs think she can't have kids. It's in the medical record." His voice is flat.

Of course she can't. That perv ruined her. My hands fist. "Who *is* this fucker?"

Noose's tight smile doesn't reach his eyes. "Arnold Jenkins. Did time for it. Sealed record because the whole mess involved a minor."

"Not sealed for you."

Noose's broadening grin is a baring of teeth. "No, not for me."

We stare at each other.

Noose searches my face. "No."

"Yes," I reply, facing off with him.

Noose is uncharacteristically casual, not picking up on my *fight me* vibe that I just spewed like pheromones. "Vipe won't want the heat. Someone smart can put his death and our involvement together, Lariat." His mercury stare lasers me. "You seeing Angel, and suddenly the foster dad from hell is toast. You feel the potential?"

My fists creak. "I want that fucking sperm stain wiped from the face of the Earth."

Noose tenses. "I hear you."

"If it were Rose—"

Noose holds up a fist. "He'd already be dead. Knotted and strung."

I bump his fist with my own, our eyes locking. "Then help me."

"Let me see what else I can dig up."

We stare at each other, and the moment drags into a full minute.

"You got something to say?" Noose asks.

But he knows.

I slowly nod, switching gears to the shit between us. It's a festering sore, and I can't stand it anymore. There's only so much emotional baggage I can carry, and I'm falling under the weight. "I blame you for those kids."

Noose's hard face softens. "Yeah, I know."

"Why'd you do it?"

Noose looks away, taking in the corner of the new club's building—a resurrected World War II bunker, which is now our headquarters in this corner of Bumfuck, Egypt.

He cocks his head to the left. "This been eating at you all this time?"

Grunting, I ask harshly, "Hasn't it you?"

Noose nods. "Mainly because it was here." He swings a palm between our bodies.

We lean against our rides, the dark sky our only witness.

"Beating the shit out of me won't bring those kids back, Dreyfus."

He uses my last name like he did when we were in.

"I know," My voice is a hoarse curse. "And that's the fucker of it. You waste the goat farmer—"

"On orders," he interjects.

I give a single, jerky nod. "Yeah, fucking orders," I say with bitterness. "I think it's false intel, and I don't have your back quick enough."

"Then the goat farmer pulls the hardware, and I knot him handily."

My hands tremble. "I had to have your back then, King. Had to. No choice, brother."

His hand lands on my shoulder and doesn't let go.

"The little one had a gun, Lariat. The smallest one of the group had a bead on me. Ya had no choice."

I cover my face with my hands. "I see their bodies dance every night. The blood's like oil. I can't get clean; I can't undo it."

"There's no bleach for the brain, brother."

I give a choking sob. My hands fist, wanting to kick my own ass.

And Noose is there, holding me while I rip chunks of my heart apart for doing ugly things—necessary things.

After a few tortuous minutes, I finally dry up and look into his hard face. "I hated you, you fucker."

A hardly-there smile hovers over his lips. "Nah. I knew it wasn't me you hated. I knew what you hated was the code. And maybe a little—yourself."

Maybe a lot. I nod miserably. "Yeah." Breath wheezes out of me, and I deflate like a balloon.

His hard hands are firm on my shoulders.

"We cool?" Noose claps me on the back, releasing me.

"After you holding me like a sissy while I bawl my eyes out? Yeah." My laugh is sad. But somewhere in there is relief, and maybe some peace.

Noose's grip is like iron on my shoulders. We're all stronger than fuck, but Noose is titanium. "You are never weak." He shakes me. "You're one of the least weak fucking men I've ever known."

Now, coming from Noose, if that doesn't make a guy feel right, nothing can.

"Okay," I finally answer.

"You got me?" Noose asks, his grip tightening to the point of pain.

"Yeah."

Noose releases me a second time, and I sit there, limp and spent. Quiet relief begins to take up the void of anger and shit I had bottled up.

"You don't think there's a day that goes by that I don't wonder if you almost died covering my ass?"

I swing my face to his in surprise. I hadn't considered it. I was too deep in my own head to get out long enough for introspection.

He nods. "Yeah." Noose lights up, cupping his hand around the flame.

Low illumination flicks on inside the club like a small startled sun. We're still whispering our secrets and unspoken terror in the dark.

"I knotted that Al-Qaeda fuck and turned." Noose's face is tilted up, seeing a different scene in the not-so-distant past. "The sky was ablaze with your fire, the roar of it."

"Their deaths."

He gives me the profile of his face. "Yeah."

Noose's smoke rings are unseen but present. The smell of his smoldering cig comforts me, and I resent quitting for the second time in a handful of days.

"That is the scene that replays in my head when I can't sleep. You being in their line of fire. Because mark my words, Dreyfus, those kids would have grown up to be used. All I could think of was that my brother hadn't died defending me for nothing."

His free hand reaches out, clutches my cut, and drags me against him. He palms my skull and shakes my head with his calloused grip. "You dumb fuck. I love ya."

It's a miracle.

Noose never says how he feels. Before Rose, if shit got raw, he used his fists. Now he uses words.

I'm getting there, but I'm not there yet.

I let his phrase hang. I can't say how I feel. I've got all I can cope with knowing what Angel went through and knowing that Noose doesn't blame me for my hesitation. He doesn't blame me for my instincts getting in the way of duty.

If only for a nanosecond.

That pause was almost too long, and losing Noose's life would have been like a thousand deaths to me.

I won't let indecision hold me back next time.

And that time is now.

I have a life that has become precious to me. I can't take back Angel's past.

But I can add a dose of justice. Lariat style.

Knots and all.

☠

"We all clear on this?"

Wring and Snare nod.

"Our guy on the inside—prison guard." Noose smirks. "All the free jail pussy he can eat." Noose turns to me "Sorry, man, no dis against Mini."

"None taken. My cousin wasn't there long enough to negotiate her body."

Snare winces, shooting a long-suffering look in Noose's direction. "You have zero tact, Noose."

He runs a hand through his hair, a cig jammed between his lips. "Yup. Sorry. I know I'm an asshole."

Silence.

"Fuck. Tough crowd." He grunts when we're still quiet. "Anyways, we'll have answers about who did Mini and why at the end of the night. But tonight is about justice."

Snare shrugs in the near dark. "Probably don't need all four of us to kill one fucking perv."

Noose nods at Snare. "Remember getting Rose, and how that mess went sideways in a heartbeat?"

Snare's face goes still, all expression wiped. "Yeah."

"Well, better safe than sorry."

"I'm in," Snare says. "I wasn't bailing." He looks at each one of us in turn. "I just don't think you badass SEALs need my untrained ass."

Wring claps him on the shoulder. "Love the company, Snare."

Noose narrows his eyes. "We want this cocksucker. Don't know what he's been doing since he got out ten years ago."

Makes me steaming pissed that he was only in prison for less than five years for raping and beating a defenseless girl.

My girl.

"Those fucks don't rehabilitate, by the way," Snare says.

He oughta know. His dad was a class A perv.

"Where does this chode live?" Wring asks. He flips his blade out, closes it, flips it out.

He's wearing knots. Wring favors small knots and lots of them. Abrasion is superior. Killing is slower with that type of rope.

I love his choices.

"Renton." Noose's answer is curt.

"Let's ride."

"Car this time," Wring says.

"Of course. Just using the phrase." Snare grins, his teeth a white slash of menace in the insulated gloom outside the club, scar effectively hidden in the gloom.

We walk over to the hot rod that Noose owns. It has strategic cancer, but the engine is mint, purring like a well-loved cat.

We pile in and head to the border of Kent and Renton—the slums. They're small-time but home to a lot of offenders.

Arnold Jenkins is no different, and he's right in the center of that particular nest of snakes.

We have his address, and now it's time to take care of business. It has been a long time coming.

I get a lot of satisfaction from delayed gratification.

19

ANGEL

Trudie's car is a stick.

Dad had promised to teach me how to drive a manual transmission. Instead, here I am, twenty-seven years old with only a ten-second lesson from Trudie under my belt. I'm spending more time killing the engine at every stoplight than actually driving.

Finally, I manage to get to Jugtner, Cognate, and Anderson. It's a few minutes before seven, and I'll be lucky to talk with everyone I need to. I'm banking on the riot of the day causing people to stay late.

I ran out of the office in an emotional whirlwind, the luxury of which I had no business succumbing to. Now, harsh reality has reared its head, and I have to make my actions right.

Palming the straight bar across the dark, reflective glass of the door to the firm, I'm momentarily blinded by a streetlamp light refracting into my eyes as it switches on.

I blink rapidly in an effort to expel the dots bursting in front of my vision as I walk through the door. As chaotic as the office was this morning, it's now as quiet as a tomb when I step into the chilled interior.

Maryanne glances up, sees it's me, and has rounded the desk before I can greet her.

She grabs my hands and tightens her grip painfully. "Angel, are you okay?" Then, before I can answer, she adds, "you left so suddenly, we couldn't figure out what was happening. And you're not answering your cell." Her lower lip trembles, and I realize I freaked everyone out.

Way to go, Angel.

"I'm sorry." I try unsuccessfully to extract my hands, but I give up and continue. "I dropped the phone when I was assaulted."

Maryanne lets go of my hands and drags a finger down the wound Tommy gave me.

The phone sitting on her desk purrs its ring in the background, and I stall out. Just on the verge of spilling everything, my lips are agape with the mess of my life.

"Hold on." Maryanne races back to the desk and flips a switch. "I'll turn it over to the service. We're at seven o'clock, anyway."

I nod and slowly sink into the couch. The day's events are catching up to me.

Maryanne tucks her sensible gray skirt underneath her knees and sits beside me. A brass tack from the pillow design on the leather couch wedges in my butt cheek, and I shift my weight. My rib twinges at the movement.

"First, I'm so sorry about Mini Dreyfus." Maryanne's pale-green eyes search my face, probably finding more than I want her to find. She shakes her head as if wanting to say more, and the sleek pewter bob haircut slithers around her softening jawline.

"Thanks."

Those strikingly pale eyes move over my wounds. "What happened to your face, Angel?"

I gulp. How much can I say? I don't want to endanger her, but I don't want to come across as a battered woman covering for a man. In my case, that would be impossible to manage, given my background. "I was mugged at Garcia's."

Maryanne's hand flies to her chest like a lost bird, her manicured short nails shining slightly under the warm white of the LED overheads. "*What?*" Her gasp is a hiss between her teeth. "Did you call the police?" Her eyebrows draw together, making a perfect number eleven between her eyes.

"No, not yet. And that's why I don't have my cell phone."

She clasps my hands again. "This is all really bad timing, Angela."

My heart sinks as I hear the other metaphorical shoe fall with a great, resounding thud.

Her lips flatten into a grim line. "I think the partners are..."

I shake my head in disbelief, my eyes burning. "I know that there will be retribution for what Lar—*Shane* Dreyfus did to Brad."

Maryanne's eyes widen, then she looks away.

It can't be good that she's avoiding my gaze.

"What?" My tone is urgent.

"I am the worst type of woman who ever lived. But you're my favorite. You're the daughter I never had. So honest, so hardworking, so hard on herself."

Her direct stare meets mine.

"You're scaring me, Maryanne."

She nods quickly. "I'm scared too."

Maryanne's sea-colored eyes pierce through me, and she takes a deep, shuddering inhalation. "The partners are going to let you go, Angel."

I slump back in the seat, dazed. I thought there was a slim possibility they would fire me due to the publicity surrounding Mini's death and the resulting connection to Lariat. The sequence of events appears sordid on the surface. But I thought since I had been with them for three years without a black mark anywhere, a little bit of explanation would remedy any wrongdoing. They would see my machinations for what they were—trying to right a wrong. That has always been my motivation.

In a way, I realize this is my fault. I was the epitome of unprofessional. I sought Lariat out on the advice of my not-so-innocent client outside of work hours.

The appearance of impropriety is there if anyone is looking closely, no matter how innocent my motives are. The mob was apparently watching my every footstep.

And though the partners can't possibly know that I had sex with Lariat, he might have illuminated our inter-action by the sheer alpha male attitude he threw around at my place of work.

He punched Brad and acted all tender when I was a shaking mess.

Maybe he's not acting, my mind whispers.

I look down at my clenched hands. From the outside looking in, he seemed genuinely disturbed by my distress. Lariat doesn't appear to keep anything in—unlike me.

So he storms in the office, sees Brad looming, and assumes the worst.

Then he kicks Brad's ass in full view of the entire office. And I somehow think Lariat's message wasn't broadcast to everyone loud and clear?

That message is simple: Angel is doing the relative of a client.

My actions—and Lariat's—cast doubt. That doubt is directed at me as a professional and as a human being capable of the quality the firm wants to represent them.

After a couple of, albeit shallow, inhales I ask, "Is there any chance?"

Maryanne's eyes tighten, and I know. "It's not my place to say."

I smile weakly. "But you already have," I say softly.

She nods. "I have, dammit." Her liquid eyes find me and trace the healing bruise on my face. "I'm sorry. From what I heard, they're giving you the minimum severance package, and you're out. They want to bury this mess. Deep."

The partners have never liked the pro bono part of the firm. If I hadn't been Gregory Monroe's daughter, I might have never gotten the opportunity to do my calling. But my role did serve them in a way. It made the firm appear philanthropic.

"What are you saying, Maryanne?" a swelling, deep baritone asks from across the room.

We simultaneously startle at the verbal intrusion.

I stand suddenly, realize I'm still entangled with Maryanne, and stumble.

Brad's smile is a slash across his handsome face; his square jaw is clenched. "I hope I didn't just hear what I think I heard?"

Maryanne dumps her gaze to the floor, tense like a rabbit caught in a snare. "No, Mr. Goren."

"Good." Brad turns his model-like face to mine.

I don't contain my gasp of shock fast enough.

"Like what your boyfriend did to my face?"

My eyes skate over the distended lump on the side of his jaw, which he just revealed by turning to face me head-on. It's a miracle Lariat didn't break his jaw. I think he meant *not* to, which is somehow scarier.

Please don't press charges, I have time to think.

"The only reason I don't go after his biker's ass is because his cousin was dispatched while under your care, and other particulars that will become apparent momentarily."

Guilt spears me, the evisceration of my psyche complete.

"I—"

Brad quells my potential rebuttal with a palm. "I know you didn't pull the trigger or whatever event took place there at felon central."

I frown. Brad is acting strangely, even in the light of most recent events.

"And you *are* dating him, aren't you, Angel?"

I whip my head back and forth, denying a dating relationship with Lariat based on general principle.

"The lady doth protest too much, methinks," Brad states quietly.

My heart starts to race, and a slow trickle of sweat rolls between my breasts.

"Maryanne," I say with slow precision. Every instinct of survival I have is lighting up like an evil Christmas tree.

"What?" she asks as though awoken from a fog.

But it's far too late. It's too late for regret, too late for understanding that all my *nos* to Brad were about something I sensed—but didn't have a concrete name for.

Brad raises a gun and points the muzzle at Maryanne.

"No!" I scream, throwing my arm forward so hard, I lock my elbow.

A soft shout of sound strikes me with quilted horror.

Skull fragments explode beside me, hitting me like small razors of bone, and I instinctively shut my eyes tight. I lift my hands to protect my face as hot blood smacks my throat and the lower part of my jaw. The pungent metallic aroma makes me involuntarily open my mouth so I don't breathe it in through my nose.

Maryanne's body falls at my feet with a thud.

I startle awake as though from a nightmare.

Brad's grin is evil. "Now *that* was satisfying."

My mouth opens and closes like a fish deprived of water.

"Cat got your tongue, slut?"

I'm not a slut, and rage-fueled adrenaline sings through me—even though Maryanne's body cools at my feet and my future is a dim hole somewhere. I don't let yet another death overwhelm me—even hers.

"I'm no slut." Shock numbs my insides, and I fight rattling apart.

He teases the gun, outfitted with a silencer, a notch higher, directing it at my face. "Stop defending your honor. We've had someone watching you since day one.

We know your goings—and we certainly know your *comings*." He enunciates that last word with a derisive sneer.

Tingling heat singes my fingertips, and my bowels hiccup, begging for release. I am literally scared shitless. But I don't know how anything fits, and my lawyer's mind struggles to align the pieces.

"Where's the rest of the staff?" I'm proud of how level I make my voice.

"It's late." He looks at the body at my feet, and I force my rising gorge down. "Maryanne"—he sighs—"the nosy bitch wanted to hang around, hoping you'd flock back so she could tell you the juicy news."

"My firing?" I ask, panic pressing in from all sides.

But panic never gets anyone anywhere. The emotion didn't help me when I was too young to fight, too fragile.

"Yes." He swings the muzzle as if it's a hand, and I resist the urge to flatten my body on the ground, eyes locked on the muzzle. "That's not important now."

"What's important?" *Keep him talking, Angel.*

"You. You're more important than you know."

Whatever. He's clearly insane. "Let me go, Brad."

Brad shakes his head. "Tried to play nice with you, but that didn't work. You'd spread your legs for whoever stopped long enough and had a dick. But *my* dick?" He makes a low noise of fury, and my body chills. "My dick wasn't good enough for our *Angel*."

I swallow. Stepping back, I trip over Maryanne's leg. My palm smacks the wall, and I hold myself up, carefully stepping backward without looking at her corpse.

I make a stab at reason with a madman. "It wasn't about your *penis*, Brad. It was about dating someone from the firm."

Did he say "*we* kept an eye on you"? I pluck the pronoun out of thin air, slotting it into my terrorized brain for later contemplation.

"I don't want to date you, Angel." His grin is feral. "I want to fuck you."

I hear a whimper and realize it's coming from me. "I'm not going to allow that."

"Here's the thing, Angel—where you're going, there's not going to be *options* about partners. Everyone's going to be a partner."

Okay. I make unsteady progress toward the door, deciding he can shoot me in the back.

"There's no escaping, Angel." His voice follows me. "Ricci is through playing cat and mouse. He's cashing all his chips in."

What chips? I don't stop my forward momentum.

"Daddy dearest fucked the wrong hole, and you're still paying the price. Actually, your pain is the bitch's pain."

"What bitch?" I ask, numbingly confused and turning to face him before I escape.

"Didn't you go to law school?"

I nod stupidly and want to kick myself.

Get out!

"What bitch?" I repeat with exaggerated slowness. It's not feigned. I really am in a miserable spot between acute shock and terror, and understanding anything has become a challenge—especially with a gun trained on me.

We're discussing riddles with Maryanne's cooling corpse between us; it's not a normal circumstance.

"Your mama." Brad taps the top of his head with the extended muzzle of the silencer, and my palms dampen at the sight.

But this has only one solution and I frown. "My mother's dead."

Brad shakes his head. "Nah, your *real* mom. The one who slept with Daddy and got knocked up." His grin is wide and genuine. "You'll have time to meet her soon. She'll *love* meeting you."

Liar. "I'm not going anywhere with you, Brad."

The door behind me, which was just out of reach, slams open, and the mob guys from the cemetery stroll in.

I recognize Talker as he takes in the dead secretary then at Brad. "Sloppy."

Brad gives an *aw shucks* grin.

"Kill yourself," he says through bared teeth.

I back up against the wall, identifying menace instantly, watching the two as though they're playing a deadly tennis match.

Brad's grin wilts around the edges.

Talker strolls toward Brad. "Put the gun to your head and blow yourself away," he repeats as if Brad is slightly stupid.

"This isn't part of the plan that Ricci outlined," Brad replies just as condescendingly.

I have to give him credit, he sounds affronted.

I would have peed myself. In fact, that's still an option.

The man draws a switchblade and puts it against Brad's crotch faster than Brad can lift the gun.

Brad's eyes bulge.

For a single, blistering moment of suspended time, I might laugh because all I can think of is Trudie's coined term, *nubby dick.*

Then the moment is gone because Talker states in a low voice, "Put the gun to your head and blow your brains out, or I slice your dick off. Your choice, Bradford."

My breath heats, and I can't move it past my lips.

Brad hesitates and meets my eyes.

He's obviously horrible, but maybe he doesn't deserve *this.*

Slowly, so slowly, he lifts his arm and does what the man instructed him to do.

I would think he would rather be alive and figure out his penisless state.

In the end, no. The report of the weapon explodes in a muffled burst. The noise of the gun is louder, at half volume, and a low ringing begins in my ears.

I stifle a sob with my hand as Brad crumples in a pile of gore. His face is half-gone. A hole in his upper jaw reveals the gleam of teeth that look like tortured Chiclets in a mouth without lips.

"That was nifty as fuck," Talker says, turning to me. "Are you going to cooperate this time, Angela?"

"No," I say through gritted teeth, my eyes wide.

He gives a sage nod. "Figured." Talker nods toward his men, and they come.

I'm trained in self-defense, one of the best—man or woman—in the classes I took for years. But I'm still no match for three men.

I thought I hurt from Tommy's surprise attack.

They rush me, and I take the first in a leading foot strike to the knee, taking out his stride from underneath him, smashing the nose of the next, but the third gets one of my arms, then the other. I'm trapped.

Their attack is so brutal an onslaught that the one who initially gave them the green light makes them back off as if he's addressing a pack of Dobermans after a bone.

This bone is hurting too badly to stay awake.

So I don't.

I try to breathe but can't. I lie gasping on the floor, figuring they've broken the ribs that were only bruised before.

Unconsciousness beats at me insistently until I can't fight it anymore. My narrowing vision sees first Maryanne then Brad. Bright red narrowing to black as it covers my brain like a thin veil of reprieve from my fright.

20

LARIAT

Drab drapes tinged with brown bow forward under murky glass that is so encased by filth, there wouldn't be a view even if the cloth was pulled back.

Thank fuck we don't need to peep through windows. That's more frontal than we would ever employ.

Our car is parked half a mile away in the open-twenty-four-hours-a-day Safeway grocery store that borders Renton like a wet dream. The highway that hugs the parking lot used to be named Benson Road, but now it's SR 515, a congested stretch that has needed to be plowed into a thoroughfare for forever.

After conferring briefly, our group splits up. There's something about four huge men dressed all in black that gets attention. And that's what we don't want tonight.

I look at this like a mission. And since there's no real arrogance in a SEAL—we all believe we're a step away from failing—that perspective keeps us sharp. As for Snare's mindset, I couldn't know. But the last time we were all together on a similar run, he felt so close to a brother in the war, I almost forgot he hadn't served. He was a natural to all the brief coaching we gave him.

Snare has earned our trust, which is no simple feat. He has been through his own war in battles he couldn't win. And when he finally won the war that mattered, he was released by his demons. The dad that had terrorized him his entire life and threatened the one woman he vowed to protect was gone.

But like us, Snare's guard never retreats. His cautious nature is a default of experience. He can't take away what he has lived no matter how much he wants to. It's part of who he is.

Like now.

Noose hikes his jaw, and I see the movement in the dark because I'm watching for it. Wring has a jet-black beanie pulled low and gives a finger signal—*move.* It's too warm a night for a cap. In the Pacific Northwest, weather cools to true autumn slowly. But Wring's platinum buzz cut is a flag of notice even in the vague light pollution of Renton.

Noose moves forward with liquid grace, which is surprising for a guy as fucking big as him.

He's at the back door of the rundown, 1950s, flat-roofed dump before I can blink.

We all follow, with Snare and me at loose center and Wring at the rear.

Noose pops the lock easily and slides through the threshold sideways. Three heartbeats later, he gives the signal for entry.

We stuff ourselves inside silently, and I flick a drop of sweat sliding from my temple to jaw. I swear it makes a *plop* sound when it hits the cracked and curling linoleum floor.

Noose had looked into this fuck. Jenkins should be at home.

He must be, judging from the blaring TV in the front room, not that speculation is fact.

Wring and Noose shoot me a glance.

I nod in return.

My kill. My plan.

I move forward, sweeping my rope, one of three, free of my pocket. The abrasive length swings with comforting weight as I slide along a wall that hasn't seen paint in two decades.

I lean my jaw along the inside corner of the wall and search the dark interior of a living room that has a strobe-like effect from the distorted colors the TV is flinging around.

A chair with an indentation as permanent as a scar is parked like a fading anchor at the room's center.

No one's in it.

Shit.

I duck on pure instinct as the simultaneous slide of a shotgun registers in my brain.

A fraction of a second later, plaster disintegrates above my head in a powder puff that cannibalizes vision.

The guys behind me are silent, and I know that something alerted Jenkins.

No time to think. Shot projectiles go wide as I go low, sweeping my leg out blindly as I do and catching the man I assume is Jenkins in the kneecap.

Lucky strike, being as how I can't see dick through the cloud of dust caused by the shot.

He howls, and Noose moves in. He aims for the guy's head and nails him in the teeth with a perfect boot plant.

Jenkins's jaw kicks back, his hand convulsing around the butt of the shotgun.

Wring is just there, yanking the weapon away at the butt.

We stand over Jenkins, his death in our faces, and he throws his hands defensively over his face.

"I didn't say nothing!" he mewls like a little girl.

Noose shoots me a puzzled look, and Snare slaps Jenkins's palms away so we can gauge his expression. "Hate to touch you, fucker," Snare comments through tight lips.

Amen.

My knot swings loose above his face, and Jenkins s eyeballs zero in on the bulbous end. Tied for size, the knot is as round as a golf ball and deadly as a flail.

"I never told nobody about her." His voice is reedy and thin with fear.

It has been my experience that everyone sounds like that on their back when begging for their life.

Wring sinks down to his haunches. Out of the bunch of us, he has the least emotional investment. Snare was raised by somebody no better than Jenkins. Noose has a daughter, so he has a different perspective now.

I can't get near Jenkins yet because he's Angel's childhood rapist. I'll kill him too soon, and I want to make it slow.

Wring gets all that shit automatically and steps in. "What are you babbling on about, Jenkins?"

"I didn't tell nobody," the man blubbers, spittle escaping from the corners of his mouth.

"Didn't tell anyone what?" Snare snarls from above him.

"About the girl."

Angel?

"What girl?" Wring's voice holds a thread of anger.

"Monroe. Who else?" he nearly wails.

Noose whips his face to mine.

I bend at the waist and grab a fistful of material by the fucker's neck, dragging every bit of his one hundred eighty pounds upright.

He's maybe five ten, and my nearly six five towers over him. "You talking about Angela Monroe?"

"Who else would I be talking about?" he squeaks within my taut hold. "I did what the boss told me."

"What boss?" I ask in a hoarse bark, resisting the urge to shake him apart by the thinnest margin of control.

He flinches. "Ricci," he whispers, his eyes searching my face for clues. *Good fucking luck with that.*

I give away nothing, releasing him before I choke him.

Jenkins staggers backward, and Snare pushes him into the wall. He slaps his hands against the wall and stares, wide-eyed and dazed, at the four of us.

"Talk. Now," Noose says.

He licks his thick lips. "Ricci sent you guys to mess me up?"

"No."

His eyes are beady and narrow. "Then who the fuck are you?"

All I can see is that stare over Angel as she struggled to get away…and never could.

My fist is suddenly flying, landing hard against his jaw. His face snaps back, colliding hard against the wall, denting it.

"Justice," I growl.

"Please stop," Jenkins pleads in a thready whisper.

Hard to talk with a partially crushed windpipe. It's a real conversation dampener.

"Tell us about why the girl was here."

Noose effortlessly tightens the knot with an expert quarter turn, and I know firsthand the pain is excruciating. After all, a man can't learn the trade unless it's turned on him occasionally.

Jenkins tries to dig the rope off his neck. An eye flick from me later, and Wring puts his full weight on Jenkins s hand.

"This pain can stop if you promise to tell us stuff," Snare says.

"Stuff?" I ask with a snort.

"Whatever," Snare says, frowning.

Jenkins jerks his head in a nod then grimaces with the movement. Noose loosens the tie. His large hands are wrapped where they need to be to finish what he started.

But I have other plans for this fuck. In fact, I don't have all the time to do all that I want to do.

"It's been fifteen years, man." His eyes are frantic between the four of us, begging us to understand. "She was *payment*. I took the girl instead of money. Old lady was on the foster list. She knew what I liked."

The mens faces take on identical ill expressions, all except Jenkins.

That fucking bitch he was married to hunted girls for him to rape. What kind of woman would aid a sick fucker like Jenkins?

"And?" Noose manages with raw disgust filling the one word.

"I offed the parents, made it look like an accident. Did a pro job. Got the Monroe girl for my efforts."

Efforts. Orphaning a little girl then systematically tearing down her soul because of his sick impulses.

"Heard enough."

Jenkins s eyes widen. "Hey, man, I told ya what happened. What are you going to do to me?" His eyes ping-pong from me to the others.

The smile I level on him is the cruelest of my life. "Everything," I answer.

The next hour is a blur of fists, blood, and retribution.

For me.

And definitely for Angel.

My knuckles are raw agony; the skin is torn clean off my dominant right hand. My fingers ache with the paces I put them through. A man who beats another to death does not escape damage.

It's hard work, physical work—and I'm tired as fuck.

Exhilarated.

We went against everything we've been trained and documented Jenkins dispatch with photographic proof.

After carefully removing the special vessels from our packs, we poured what we brought with us over his body,

The chemical cocktail dissolves Jenkins's body on contact. When the acidic mix eats away at the floor, the bloodied soup that had been Jenkins collapses into the shallow crawl space below.

Gasoline is tossed with precision on the lower floor like toxic rice at a wedding.

But this is no ceremony. Everything is a grim task.

We leave as silently as we came.

Wring strikes the match as we depart. The flame lights, standing up like a bright torch against the dark house, where we'd just made the world slightly better than it had been three hours ago.

Wring flicks the lit match, and it arcs, landing perfectly in the threshold of the battered door. It flares in a burst, seeking the line of fuel like a blue flame licking a highway.

Noose faces me, and for a heartbeat, the inferno illuminates his face, making him resemble a demon.

We turn and, without communication, yoke into the surrounding soft black of night.

"That was a *thing*," Snare comments, flopping into Noose's car.

We don't reply.

After a few tense minutes of silence as Noose navigates us east toward the club, I ask, "You got the stuff we needed when I was working Jenkins over?"

"Yeah."

I turn toward Snare, my eyes trained to the murk of the backseat from the front, cataloging his micro expressions. "You got a problem with how things went down?"

Snare shakes his head. "No." He lifts a hand and lets out a rough exhale. "Yeah."

Noose cocks his head from the driver's seat, his eyes pegging Snare like a bug on a board. "Speak now or forever hold your fucking peace, brother."

Snare is visibly shaken.

"What is it?" Wring asks, casually picking at his nails. There's not one casual thing about any of us.

"You guys—what the *fuck* was that shit you used on Jenkins?"

Wring murmurs, "Bye-bye-gone—no evidence."

"You don't give a shit about Jenkins, do ya?" Noose asks with a sharp lilt, his light brows pulling together.

"Nah. Forget him as a human being. He raped a little girl as payment for murdering her parents. He deserved it. I just—fuck, that was *so* goddamned ugly."

"Nope," Wring says with calm precision. "That's chemistry, my friend. And Lariat showed a bit of mercy." He tips his blade up, the metal glinting softly from the occasional streetlamp that tosses light inside the car as it rolls toward the club.

Snare shifts his attention from Wring to me. "Because you only used your rope at the end?"

I shake my head, and Wring and I exchange a glance. I can feel Noose's gaze on me instead of the road.

I know my eyes are pits of indifference inside my head, no effort needed. "No. Because I used the make-him-disappear juice when he was already dead."

"Jesus," Snare says, covering his face with a hand.

No one can say I don't have compassion.

Jenkins's murder would never give me nightmares—*not* ending him would have.

21

ANGEL

The water is frigid in my face, as though someone is punching me with a block of ice.

My eyes snap open. Water droplets cling to my eyelashes. I can't connect what my vision is telling me with what I'm seeing.

I'm strapped to a chair, every bit of me in some degree of pain.

Opposite me is a woman that looks to be a very well-preserved fifty.

I blink the water away, searching automatically for the thrower.

I find him.

Talker, the one who killed Brad, is holding an empty bucket in one hand.

I say nothing, and he smiles. His dark hair is slicked back from his face, and a bare bulb in the ceiling gives his pockmarked skin a slightly green pallor. "*There* she is. You finally joining us, Angela?"

I don't reply, but my gaze goes back to the woman. I'm so hurt, I can barely breathe through it. Every inhale feels like breathing through crushed glass.

Ribs. Broken.

Face. Beaten.

I would assess the damage, but it doesn't matter. Zip ties are wrapped around my ankles and wrists. My depth perception is off because one of my eyes is swollen shut. *Marvelous.*

I am so broken up, I try to muster fear and just feel tired instead. Maybe I can get him to kill me.

I think of Lariat, and instant sadness crushes me. I know it's not logical that I can fall in love with another human being in less than a week. Since I was twelve, I've had to live mainly in survival mode. My experiences have raised the bar on my other senses. And I think I might have an advantage on some of humanity because of what I've been through.

Lariat woke something in me I thought I had lost.

Hope.

And now it's gone. In its place is determination.

My one good eye moves back to the woman. Her face swims within my compromised vision.

Then I see it and stifle my shock badly. Her eyes are the same color as mine.

I've never met anyone with my eye color before.

I get asked all the time if my eyes are hazel, gold, or green. No one knows. I put hazel on my driver's license, but it's a lie. There isn't a designator for my eye color. Gray is as exotic as they allow at the DMV.

And there's no explanation that covers how weird it is to be beaten to a pulp and look across the room at the person I understand on an almost primal level to be my mother.

I grieved for a woman who wasn't my mother.

"Here's your big chance, Maria. Make good on it."

The woman shoots him a glance of pure hatred.

I know exactly how she feels.

"Hello, Angela." Her rich contralto voice washes over me, and suddenly, I want to cry.

But I won't. Here is somebody else who could have come for me when I needed protection.

And didn't.

"As you might have already guessed, I am your real mother."

"Yes," I say, boring cavern-like holes into her skull with one eyeball.

She fists the material of her navy pencil skirt then smooths her hands over the material and meets my eyes again. Black hair, with fine gray strands like tinsel falls forward, partially hiding her face.

"Your father loved me," she begins, and I want to rail against her. I saw how my father loved my mother. What they had wasn't feigned.

"The woman you believed to be your mother...was your aunt."

They were married. Memories jumble inside my addled brain. *No, no, no.*

She holds up a palm. "It isn't what you think. He was protecting her. They were hiding in plain sight, if you will. They thought they'd escaped the family."

Mafia.

"When really, it was only a matter of time. They posed as a married couple, and that gave them an extended hiatus without violence, without fear."

Memories of my dad kissing my mother's cheek surface. Every intimacy I witnessed had not been sexual, I dimly realize.

She lifts her delicate chin, her bone structure so similar to my own. "I was sent to seduce him."

My fingers close into fists, straining the tight plastic. "Why?"

"I was to do it, or I would die," she says simply. "It was the ultimate revenge. Get Greg to love me. Then I became pregnant with his child." Her eyes slide away then return to mine. "When I became pregnant, he knew he couldn't divorce his sister. Their false marriage was keeping her alive. It was keeping her away from who she was supposed to be married to."

"Who?" I ask, though I'm certain.

"Antonio Ricci."

"Shit," I say with a painful exhale. My mind spins as I put everything together.

"So she was supposed to marry Ricci, and my father—her brother—helped her escape an arranged marriage by marrying her under a false name?"

She nods. "Then, as a cruelty to me, he saw to Greg and Libby's deaths. That left you vulnerable."

Horribly vulnerable. She has no idea.

Or maybe she does. My eyes narrow.

"We know about Arnold Jenkins, Angela."

Her admission is like a sucker punch. My already shallow breathing becomes shallow scoops of oxygen on the surface, and I can barely breathe. Stars burst at the fringe of my vision like firecrackers.

"He was part of the example to the family. Deserters will be punished. Being female or being a child, or both, is not enough of a deterrent to keep it from happening."

Ricci had my parents killed then made sure I was placed with that raping monster.

I throw up without warning. One second, I'm dissecting the treachery surrounding my life, and the next, pain explodes in my midsection as my abused ribs shriek and I evacuate Trudie's delicious lasagna I ate hours ago.

"I don't think I can stand this, Dean."

Dean, the Talker and he of the throwing ice water at bound women, narrows eyes so pale they look like dirty window glass. Hands knotted, he flexes his powerful arms behind his back. "Tough. I got my instructions."

"She's my daughter. And regardless of the example they've made of her, Angela doesn't deserve this. Untie her. See to her injuries."

"I don't give a fuck about her. She's just another crack I put marks on and get to stick my dick in."

God. Vomit dribbles out of my mouth, and a second wave tries to claim me.

I beat the urge down viciously. It's not so hard, considering how awful I feel.

I've felt worse. Everything I suffer now is measured to *before,* the terrifying misery of Jenkins. And still—broken ribs, beaten body, and one awful revelation later, it's all still better than *before.*

My bio-mom stands, facing off with the mob fucker. "Ricci said that once she was captured, we could have a relationship."

Not possible.

My parents might not have been perfect, and the woman posing as my mom may have really been my aunt. But she loved me better than a dozen real moms.

That memory is pure, and I don't want the taint of another superimposed over it. I lift my chin. "Don't bother; it's too late. Jenkins made sure of that."

She flinches as though I'd hit her. "I begged Ricci not to let you be in that man's care."

His care. *His brutality, you mean.*

I clamp my lips shut. "And what stopped you from protecting me?"

Dean's sullen silence stands between us, making the chasm seem even wider.

"Ricci said he'd kill me, and I'd never have a chance to be your mother. That an example had to be made so no one would ever be able to escape tradition again." Her voice ends in a whisper.

"How'd that work out?" I spit through my pain.

A single tear brims on her eye, so close a color to my own that it's like looking in a mirror. "Badly." But her chin lifts, and I see myself tucked in there for an instant. "However, I think things just got better."

She smiles and turns calmly to Dean. She extracts her hand from behind a single pleat in her skirt and puts a bullet in his brain.

The retort shoots pain into my ears, and I clench my teeth to keep from screaming.

Dean's brains decorate the wall behind him, sliding down the surface behind his body like a slow-moving mass of bright red sludge. The thicker bits cling to the soup that was his brain.

I swallow another urge to puke as my real mother calmly pivots and walks toward me.

Oh my God. *Oh my God.*

"It's okay now, Angela."

I shake my head. "Just kill me now. If you ever felt anything for me, just end me so I don't have to…" I close my eyes, dying inside—saying the words anyway. "So I don't ever have to be touched against my will again."

Her voice comes so close to my ear, I recoil. "I'm not here to kill you."

I open my eyes slowly. Her own are inches from my face. "I've been waiting for the right moment for years. And I don't care if I die anymore. Your life is worth more than my own."

She sets the gun carefully on the bare concrete floor and extracts a knife from the pocket of her skirt.

I suck in a breath.

But instead of hurting me, she cuts through the bindings.

I fall forward, and she catches me.

I want to squirm away, but I realize I can't move. I can't feel my arms or legs yet. My lungs feel crushed.

"Broken ribs," I say in a low voice.

Her smile is bright, satisfied. "You hurt the other men quite badly."

My smile is pained but genuine as I remember deci-mating knees and noses. "Good."

"Can you walk?" she asks.

No. I nod.

I lurch to my feet, and she tucks me under her arm.

"You're tall," I say in surprise.

"Yes."

I awkwardly turn, scabbing onto her blouse, my eyes bulging slightly. "They'll have heard the gunshot."

She shakes her head, and I notice how beautiful she is.

"Soundproof."

My relief wheezes out of me. "Okay."

We make our way across the room. I'm shuffling as she practically drags me behind her.

Finally, we get to the solid steel door, and she raps a patterned knock on the surface.

It opens wide, and one of the men who beat me senseless appears. Tape covers his nose where I broke it, and when he speaks, his voice is damaged.

Must have been that esophagus love I gave him with my knuckles.

His expression is clearly puzzled. "Bethany—what?"

My bio-mom had picked up the gun as we walked to the door. She parks the muzzle comfortably against the man's head and pulls the trigger.

A black hole appears in his forehead, brains shooting out like a reverse cannon as half his face disintegrates in a cloud of gore.

I slowly blink, breathing shallowly out of my mouth. It hurts, but I can't breathe through my nose.

Keep it together, Angel. Don't lose it now.

The guy sort of staggers backward, like a zombie without a plan, and tips over, landing with a plank-like thud on the floor behind him.

"Okay?" my mother asks in an unaffected voice.

I give a shaky nod.

"We're going to step over Harold and make our way outside. We're almost there, Angel."

I want to ask her not to use my nickname, but since she appears to be saving me, I'll hold off. Besides, I'm too hurt to argue.

She guides me carefully over the top of Harold, and the narrow corridor appears to grow longer as we travel the length.

I've never made such a long journey in my life. By the time we reach the end, I'm a sweating, shaking mess.

She presses the door open, and blissful fresh air hits me like a salve. The other man who I remember punching me in my face over the same wound Tommy gave me rises with an obvious limp from a metal folding chair.

His eyes drill me, and his big, meaty hands fist as though he's ready for a re-do. "What the—"

"Hi," Bethany says in a breathy voice and shoots him at point-blank range.

The movement jars my ribs, and I moan, even as half of his head blows off, sounding like a burst watermelon as it lands on the asphalt and only his mouth and part of his sheered off nose remain.

By now, I'm pretty sure I'm deaf. Bethany's mouth is moving—forming words—but all I can hear is a sharp ringing. All I can smell is the scent of gunpowder and metal.

But I'll be deaf and alive, I have time to think.

Then Tommy's there, behind her, a gun in his hand.

My eyes widen at him, and that's the only warning I have time to give to this woman who gave birth to me.

A hole blooms like a red flower in her upper chest.

Hands sliding down the front of me, she clings. Earnest eyes of bright chartreuse gaze up at me. "I... loved you—Angel."

I didn't realize I was in any shape to hold her, but I do.

We sink together, and her hair falls across my lap like a black fall of water.

"No," I choke.

Tommy is moving toward us. His smile tells me he thinks we're sitting ducks. I know I must look like hell, and he shot Bethany.

I move my hand to cover the gun she still has her finger hooked around.

Her eyes move to mine and hold.

I flick my glance upward. Tommy is almost on us.

His attention is so focused on my face that he doesn't notice my subtle movement.

Dammit, I can't get her finger out of the trigger!

Then Tommy's head lists sideways.

Something is around his neck—a small rope of some kind. Many knots decorate the length of it with exacting separation.

The noose jerks.

The crunch of Tommy's neck breaking fills the space.

I sit there, hardly breathing, with my dying mother in my arms.

Hurt, confused, and afraid, I stare as Tommy appears to slowly collapse in on himself.

Revealing Lariat.

I hiccup back a sob I'm too injured to make.

He smiles, letting the body drop, and steps over it, coming to me.

Coming for me.

22

LARIAT

"I want answers!" I roar into the closed space.

"Calm the fuck down!" Noose bellows back, veins standing out at equal attention on his thick throat. "I told you—we don't know what happened. Only that Angel was at her office, shots were fired, cops are crawling the scene, and that pretty boy attorney shot himself."

I jerk my chin up from glaring at the floor and stare at Noose. "That guy loved himself. I knew that inside five seconds of meeting him. There's no way he'd off himself."

"That's not entirely accurate. You didn't meet him— your fists did." Noose folds his arms, eyelids lowering to look at me through a slanted mercury gaze.

I shrug, then grit out, "Where's Angel?"

Snare blasts into church, a grin riding his face, causing the scar he has to buckle over his upper lip. "Got someone who saw Angel."

"Snare—"

"Settle, brother." His grin widens. "They're not far. And you'll never believe where they've hidden her."

I'm in no mood to guess. Angel's in trouble. She didn't do what the fuck I said and stay put at her girlfriend's. Every minute we waste is a minute they can hurt her.

He tells me, and my mouth gapes. "The old clubhouse?"

"Beautiful," Wring says. "We can be there inside ten minutes."

I'm already striding for the door. "Less."

☠

I'd been going off half-cocked, when the brothers forced me to slow down long enough to form a game plan.

We had leased the last place, and it had been a shithole. It's the very reason we decided to restore the World War II bunker. We paid cash. It belonged to Road Kill MC free and clear.

As we pull up a few blocks from the old digs, we kill the car's engine. It's the second time today we didn't use our bikes. We don't want to announce ourselves. We also didn't temp fate by carrying.

We are carrying, but nothing of the bullet-and-metal variety, but of rope and skill—with a chaser of vengeance.

Snare takes rear point, and compared to my ex-SEAL teammates, he's loud as we approach the old clubhouse.

A beaten Angel appears, half-falling out of the main entrance's solid steel door. Instantly, my brain starts running through the floor plan of the place, thinking of the sound-proofed rooms and wondering if Angel was held there.

When I survey the shape she's in, adrenaline sweeps through me in an extremity-tingling, nauseating surge.

My eyes instinctively scan the area and halt on the fucker I already tap danced on, Tommy.

He raises a gun.

I start sprinting before I think not to.

Angel is leaning against an older woman who looks strikingly like her.

I won't make it. I pour on speed.

Tommy's shot goes slightly wide and punches through the other woman's shoulder.

The impact causes her to fall.

Angel is so hurt, she reacts by collapsing to the ground beside the older woman. She somehow manages to drag the woman onto her lap.

As I race across the shoddy pavement with my brothers' stealthy tread echoing in my ears, I jerk a length of knotted rope out of my pocket.

Tommy's body tenses as he hears or senses me positioning behind him.

I loop the knot with my right hand and catch the tail with my left then jerk it taut.

He makes a satisfying gasp as I set the central knot beneath his Adam's apple.

Tommy struggles, and that helps me tighten the hasty noose I just made.

Blood pools toward us on the pavement from the injured woman.

But I'm in the zone.

I'm not thinking about Angel, the other woman, my safety, or the future.

The only things on my mind are my hands and the knot.

My pressure application is steady, and I feel when Tommy's trachea collapses. I hold, counting the seconds, my posture like steel, my intent resolved.

I feel the true weight of his body as death claims him.

My left hand releases the tail, and it unwinds from my wrist.

Tommy slides, giving himself a post-mortem re-break as his nose smacks the ground.

My eyes move to Angel as she holds the bleeding woman. Her uninjured eye finds me.

I see a lot in that one, shimmering orb.

Maybe it's not wishful thinking after all—me believing we have something deep.

Our locked gaze doesn't break. It looks as though she might love me. A little.

"Lariat," she whispers, choking back a sob of relief that's so obvious, the sound tightens my own throat with emotions.

Angel holds her arms up. Carefully, I bend over and set the older woman gently on the ground then lift Angel into my arms.

Nothing has ever felt better.

Doc wipes his hands and carefully walks around the bed where Angel is sleeping. It's not a real bed, more of a glorified cot.

But her face is peaceful. It should be; she's doped to the max.

"Not gonna lie. Haven't ever had to patch a woman up like this."

I'm not a crier, but seeing her delicate beauty beaten off her body is almost more than I can fucking bear. I cup my hand over my face and scrub over it about four times, gaining a shaky control over my shit. "Fuckers." I grind the word out.

"Sounds like the other woman took care of them," Doc says with an impressed snort.

My gaze travels to the mystery woman on a cot identical to Angel's. A needle is inserted in the crook of her arm, and a yoked metal rod holds two bags—one clear and one red.

"She's actually in decent shape. Bullet is a through and through." He shrugs. "Got a bag of blood, maybe two, and she's clear."

"Angel?" I ask.

Doc shakes his head, bushy eyebrows rising. "Aside from the fact that you interrupted my porn viewing?"

Wring's lips tweak. "Old perv."

"Yup." He folds his arms. "I don't think I'll get it up for a month after tallying your old lady's injuries."

"Just tell me," I say in a low voice, not correcting the old lady reference.

Doc sighs. "Two broken ribs. Set her nose." He eyeballs me, and I nod. "Fine. A broken finger, one nail missing. Strained wrist." His eyes travel to Angel's still form. "Looks like she pressed her body into service it couldn't provide. Strained her own wrist handing out the discipline. Her injuries are consistent with some men I've seen in hand-to-hand combat."

"Except she's a woman."

He nods. "Yes. Pound for pound, if she were fighting for her life, adrenaline would have seen her through what she was dishing out. But part of her injuries are from what she did to those men."

"Good," Noose says curtly. I know what he means. It's not good that she's all fucked up, but it's good that she dished out some hurt.

"Yeah." Snare jerks a thumb Noose's way. "I hope she Fucked. Them. Up."

"Oh, she did," Doc says with surety. "But they hurt her back."

"What else?"

"She's not going to lose the eye, but she won't see with it for a little while. Needs a specialist."

I close my eyes. The thought of not being able to look into both of her gorgeous eyes is brutal.

Doc claps my shoulder. "She's all over the news, Lariat. We got to get her to the cops. Make this blow up big time. The only way to protect Angela Monroe is for everyone to know what happened."

"They'll come after the MC."

He shakes his head. "No. We prime the pump, and everything will be just fine."

Viper walks in, looks around, and his eyes shift to the injured women. "They okay?"

Doc nods. "Older broad has a flesh wound. I've doped them to the hilt."

He nods. "Good." His pale-blue eyes work the room, taking in all the brothers. When they come to me, he says, "Clusterfuck."

I nod. "Yeah."

Vipe walks to me and puts a hand on my shoulder. "You did the right thing, son. I'm proud of you."

It's what I needed to hear, and I didn't know it. My throat closes up, my eyes burn, and all I can do is nod.

"Now let's figure our way out of this mess."

The brothers ignore my struggle, thank fuck.

"We can brief Angel on what to say. She can claim amnesia, blackout—whatever." Snare hikes his shoulders, the stiff leather cut he wears creaking with the motion.

"She'll have to," Wring says.

Trainer pipes in. "Can she get in trouble for lying? I mean, they're gonna find the rope burns on that mob guy."

Noose groans. "Angel doesn't have to lie; she just doesn't say that part."

Trainer pulls a face of pure confusion.

"Gotta be bright to lie well," Wring adds.

That takes Trainer out of a lot of shit that Road Kill does. But he's loyal and decent. I answer him, speaking my own thoughts aloud. "We'll get Angel to say what happened, put the heat where it belongs. On Ricci. Since the only witness was killed so publicly, the media will be all over that. We can bury the rest."

The room stills when a hushed voice calls my name.

It's the only voice that matters.

One gorgeous eyeball finds me, and I stride to Angel's side. "Baby," I say, emotion so strong, I can hardly get the word out.

"I'm that bad, huh?" she asks after half a minute of studying my face.

No lies. Not with her.

I nod.

A tear squeezes out of her one eye.

I cup the back of her skull. "How do you feel?"

She gives a defeated laugh, then her face pinches from the pain.

"Doc," I call urgently.

She gives a minute shake of her head. "No more drugs. I-I want to be awake."

I nod.

"She can have more, or we can get her freshened up and somewhere safe," I say.

Our eyes meet, and she gives a tiny nod.

I know just the place.

"Holy fuck," Trudie cries when she sees Angel in my arms.

I say, "It's better than it looks."

Trudie's light-brown eyes go to my face. "Bring her in, and then we're going to talk."

After I gently set Angel on the bed in the spare bedroom, I sit with Trudie.

She sits in the God-awful purple chair, and I perch on the edge of a fragile flowery couch.

I start at the beginning, and when I reach the end, she leans back against the chair.

"I was there, Lariat. I lived with Angel when she came out of that place."

I smile. "She doesn't ever have to worry about Arnold Jenkins again."

Trudie looks at me for a long time. "I don't think she's going to have to worry much anymore. Right, stud?"

I nod, lips curling. "Yeah."

"I knew I liked you."

"So can you be here for her? I gotta lie low."

"Absolutely."

I hand her my contact info.

She closes her fingers around it. "If she wants to get in touch with you, she does." Her unspoken question of *choice* is looking for confirmation, and I inhale deeply, letting out the breath with excruciating slowness.

Angel's got to *want* to be with me.

I nod again, because God knows if I say anything else, it'll be to beg for Angel to call me the instant she's better and to come live with me.

Love me.

So I don't say anything. I stand instead, walk to the door, and let myself out.

Hardest. Fucking. Thing. Ever.

23

ANGEL

I tie my fingers together. They shake so badly, they're distracting me from my testimony.

The judge nods for me to continue.

My eyes try to lock onto the judge, but my injury has made the one eye lazy.

Thoughts of the beating come rushing back.

I'm in physical therapy, but every time I hear a sudden noise, I have to refrain from peeing my pants. My armpits tingle with sweat, and my heart palpitates.

In a nutshell, I'm a mess.

They call it PTSD. But I've never been in a war. I just know that I feel so fragile now, like a figure made of blown glass.

"Miss Monroe," the judge encourages.

My good eye tracks his kind eyes, and the other... well, the other tries. "Yes, thank you—I'm not. I'm sorry."

Tears threaten, and I breathe deeply, concentrating only on that.

"Take your time. No one will rush your testimony."

"Thank you, Your Honor." I don't look at the stenographer or anyone else. I pretend I'm alone.

I pretend I'm at my parents grave. "As I was saying," I begin again, pushing a strand of hair out of my face, "I came to, and my mother—"

"Alleged," the defense lawyer interjects.

"I'll allow that, but let's keep interruptions to a minimum." We all hear the warning in his voice.

My fingers find each other again and start twisting. "Anyway, she's bleeding, and Tommy—"

"Thomas Bernard, alleged Ricci associate," a disembodied voice flatly states for the record.

"Yes," I say without looking up. "Tommy is going to shoot again. Shoot me," I whisper. Gooseflesh creeps over my skin at the recitation.

"What happens then, Miss Monroe?"

I think of the simplicity of the story—the lie by omission of the truth.

I raise my eyes and speak it easily. "I'm not entirely sure." I give a helpless little shrug, no acting required. "The next thing I recall is being at my friend's house, where she called the police."

Lawyers sharp eyes crawl over my face.

But my duplicity is bone-deep. I'm not giving Lariat up.

Ever.

THREE MONTHS LATER

"That's it, Angel—keep tracking."

"I hate you," I say, my bad eye aching like a rotten tooth.

The physical therapist's kind eyes crinkle at the corners. "I get that a lot. Thankfully, sweet talking never seems to work."

He moves the ball ceaselessly, left then right.

I blink, and it lasts four seconds as my bad eye weeps behind my closed lid.

"Angel."

My eyelid springs open, and I wipe the leaking away with a swift hand. Then the lid starts twitching.

"We'll wait through the spasm."

This one lasts thirty seconds.

When it's done, Lawrence pats my knee. "That's good enough for today."

I sit up, and my ribs sing from the movement. I don't touch myself anymore to take stock of my injuries. I'm healing.

But my psyche is a different thing.

I'm scared—because of what I want and because of what I don't want to lose.

"How's your vision?"

"Excellent."

Lawrence nods, tapping my chart. "Another month of PT, and you should be able to do all this fun at home."

My lips twist in a wry smile. "The torture."

Lawrence leans forward, his teeth very white within his brown face. "Feel lucky you didn't do anything to your knee. That takes a degree of commitment." His voice is bland.

I shudder.

"You're seeing everything fine, then? Just muscle control is still weak?"

"I see everything great."

I see so much now.

"See you next week, Angel."

I stand and walk out the door.

Vision restored.

Bravery in question.

But bravery and stupidity are nearly the same thing.

I decide I would rather be stupid and know than be brave and let pride get in the way.

I'm so nervous, my hand covers my stomach to measure my breaths.

The media frenzy has died down, and I don't get calls all day with questions I don't want to answer.

Questions like—"How does it feel to know that Arnold Jenkins is missing and presumed dead?"

Good, I answer in my mind before I disconnect.

Or—"How does it feel to know your parents' death was no accident?"

Terrible.

And my favorite—"What will you do now that Antonio Ricci is on death row?"

Celebrate.

Eventually, I became weary and changed my number.

My thoughts vaporize as the air becomes charged with electricity, and I know that means *he* has walked into Garcia's.

Our eyes meet in the mirror that lines the backsplash of the bar, where colorful liquor bottles fill the shelf in front of it, and I offer a shy, weak smile.

Lariat doesn't smile, and my breath catches.

He prowls to me, and I turn on the stool, my high-heeled sandal hooked on the circle of metal at its base.

Lariat doesn't stop. His eyes run from the top of my head to my toes.

I'm plucked off the edge of the stool and in his arms before I take my next breath.

His lips crash into mine. The kiss is ferocious.

Any concern of audience or public displays of affection are tossed out the metaphorical window.

Lariat comes up for air, and I try for cool. "Miss me?" I ask with a shaky laugh.

"Like food," he growls and kisses me again, savoring my lips like a gourmet delicacy.

His nearness makes me dizzy.

"Let's take this somewhere," he says.

I nod because speech isn't possible.

My cheeks heat as he tows me out of the bar and grill where we first met.

Everyone stares as we walk out. But Lariat doesn't care.

And that's good enough for me.

The bike ride is cold, so I huddle at his back, my arms wrapped around his flat, hard stomach, hanging on for dear life.

We ride south through the Kent valley, eventually heading east toward Orting.

Finally, after a really long zigzagging drive, we pull up in front of an old-fashioned-looking two-story house. To the left and right, a couple of other houses can be seen in the distance—close enough to see but far enough away to give us privacy.

Night has fallen. This far away from the city, the sky is a shroud of black with early stars beginning to glitter like forgotten gems in the dark.

Lariat shuts off the bike, and I put my hand on his shoulder. I awkwardly stand on the secondary pegs my feet were resting on and swing a leg over.

His large hand shoots out, and I take it. He easily swings me off the seat with a strong hand.

Lariat's dismount is smooth and unassuming. Hardly more than a looming, muscled dark shape, he reaches for me, and we meet as though we've rehearsed a dance step to perfection.

"Trudie told me," I say.

"I waited," he replies simply.

I plant my forehead on his chest, feeling the steady beat of his heart.

"Are you okay?" Lariat asks. His deep voice reverberates through the bones of my skull.

"Do I look okay?" I'm suddenly afraid that my faded bruises, beat-up body, and eyeball will matter.

"Fuck yes." He chuckles, cupping my jaw. "More than okay. *Fine.*"

I tip my chin up, and he cradles my face then kisses my lips so softly that it's like heated breath.

"Where are we?" I ask between his kisses.

He sweeps his arm toward the house. "My new place."

My eyes scan the house. "Looks old-fashioned."

"Supposed to."

He holds my hand as we walk slowly up the broad stairs. A low-wattage LED shines over the front door, which is painted a bright, cherry red.

I run my fingertips over the bright paint. "That's pretty."

"I like color."

I cock my head, giving him amused eyes. "Apparently."

Lariat taps in a code on the numbered entry pad, and it chimes. He depresses the oil-rubbed bronze handle, which is shaped in a hammered swirly style, and walks in.

"Oh my God," I whisper in awe.

Cool sage walls run from the entry into an open living room. Deep chocolate sectional couches with a lounger at one end have a rich, soft suede finish. My eyes are everywhere at once but come to a screaming halt at the kitchen.

Knotty alder cabinets make a bold visual statement, riding to the ceiling in elegance. Tumbled travertine flows from the back of the countertop to undercabinet, abutting a cream and mocha quartz countertop that's a wave of warmth.

The whole kitchen is beautiful and elegant.

I turn to Lariat, and his black gaze is hooded. "Like what you see?"

I nod slowly. "I…" My eyes travel to my hands, and I'm so damn grateful that my bad eye isn't choosing this moment to have a spasm. "I don't know what this means, Lariat."

I hold out my hands in front of me without looking, and he instantly takes them.

"It means I've had a shit-ton of time to figure out what I want. Who I want."

I look up when I hear the low command in his voice. "I'm a mess," I say, half-talking him out of what I think he'll say.

He laughs, softly shaking his head.

"We'll be a mess together."

"I'm unemployed." The firm didn't bow to public pressure to take me back. Two murders and my association with Lariat nixed that possibility.

"Fuck them. We got a club lawyer who's about ready to retire."

"Who? Where?" I feel my brows pull together.

Lariat chuckles. "Probably the Bahamas, if he's smart."

My laugh is tinny. "I don't sleep anymore. Every loud noise I hear makes me want to…" I pull my hands from his hold and cover my face.

He leans down and peels my hands away.

"Let's try, Angel. Tell me that you met with me because you want this thing that was between us."

I want it so, so badly. Tears pour out of my eyes. My wish for a bit of happiness consumes me. I stop breathing, and my heart pounds.

"Breathe," Lariat says.

I take measured breaths. Finally, I give him my answer.

It's not a word, but a touch.

One of many.

We crash into the wall, and like before, he braces me. "This okay, baby?" Lariat asks between ragged breaths. "Don't want to hurt you."

I am so not hurting. I wrap my hands around his thick neck and hike up the front of him.

Lariat grabs my ass cheeks and lifts me, taking me into what I assume is his bedroom.

Gently, as if I'm made of glass, he sets me on the bed.

He grins, eyeing me over. "Hair's blown to shit."

I pop the clip off my hair, and it falls around my body. The wisps at my temples are slightly snarled.

Lariat's eyes darken, and he sinks to the end of the bed, slowly unbuckling my sandals. They fall to the floor with a soft thump. He runs his rough hands up the smooth skin of my shins, and when he gets to the hem of the impractical skirt I chose, he pauses.

"You sure?"

I widen my legs, and he groans. His finger goes to my center and slips under the edge of my panties.

My head kicks back as I moisten from his touch.

As rough and passionate as our other sex was, this is tender and slow.

He rises to his knees, jerks his shirt off by the collar, and tosses it on the floor.

I lift my arms, and he rolls my thin sweater over my breasts, pausing at my nipples. He thumbs them softly as he continues. They pebble, begging for a second touch.

He tosses my sweater on top of his discarded shirt and leans over my breast, sucking softly through the lace.

I moan, and his hands run down my ribcage.

"Better?" His seriousness cools the passion slightly between us.

"Yes."

Then he makes me forget that I was nearly beaten to death only three months before.

My rapist is gone.

And Ricci is not going anywhere; his particular family is broken.

So many hurts erased, so much joy to gain.

Soft kisses rain down from the bottom of my lace-encased breasts to my belly button. Then my panties are sliding off my hips, and his tongue is at my center.

My hips buck, and he holds me still with a forearm. "Want to hear your noises, Angel."

I make them because I can't help myself. I'm frantic for him. Only for Lariat.

With the next sweep of his tongue, I explode around him. A soft scream escapes my lips as my channel pulses.

"That's it, baby."

In the next moment, his jeans are gone, and a huge erection bobs as he knee-walks between my legs, seating himself where he needs to be.

Slowly, so slowly, he enters me, and I arch to meet him, smoothly rising as he sinks inside me.

My wet welcome to his thrusting is repeated, our flesh smacking and parting. A beautiful heat begins to build, and a second orgasm hits me, sweeping through me, through us. Lariat's smooth rhythm stops, and he's suddenly pounding me as I meet each thrust.

His body stiffens, and he shouts my name, frozen above me in a moment of unreal male perfection.

Lariat's eyes find mine. He must not be sure of what he sees there.

I'm not sure, either. But I know right now that I'm content, happy, and deliriously tired. I feel as though the heartache, exhaustion, and uncertainty of the last three months have just crashed down.

"Come ere." He scoops my healing body against his hard one.

I fight to stay awake. In the end, I can't. I'm safe and warm because of Lariat's presence.

I'm happy.

EPILOGUE
ONE YEAR LATER

Mine.

Can't get over that one word. Never really felt as if I belonged to anyone but myself and the team.

This last year hasn't been easy. Angel was traumatized.

But I know trauma.

I never thought I would be a hero who mattered to anyone.

I roll over on the bed and survey my wealth. It's not money and shit. I have plenty of that.

It's this gorgeous creature who sleeps beside me each night.

I trace my eyes over her body. When that's not enough, I use my fingertips.

Angel comes awake with a smile I can't live without. I know my smile is pussy-whipped, and I don't give a shit.

She's my Angel. Mine.

"How you feeling, baby?"

"Pretty good for a fat cow."

I smirk. Angel is *not* a fat cow. She is very, very pregnant. My fingers splay over her large, swollen belly, and an elbow—or maybe a foot; hell if I know—kicks at my hand.

A surprised laugh shoots out of me. "That kid's gonna be a bruiser."

She takes my hand and brings it to her mouth then kisses the center of my palm.

"Just like his daddy."

My heart swells, and I feel as if it will bust out of my chest.

"Let's grab breakfast."

She nods then sort of can't get out of the bed. I hoist Angel, and she waddles after me into the kitchen—our kitchen.

She sold her place. We got hitched about half a year ago and moved her into my place.

Doctors said she couldn't have kids because of what Jenkins did to her, so Angel ditched the shot habit.

Turns out they were wrong.

I wrap my arms around her tightly, pulling her in close. "I got something to show you."

She turns curious eyes to me. The bad one cooperates about ninety-nine percent of the time.

If I could turn back time, I would kill those fuckers again.

But Angel's real mom did a stand-up job.

"What?" she asks.

"I'll show you before food. Hoping you'll still have your appetite. I want the shit off my phone too."

Now I've really got her full attention.

Angel follows me slowly into the living room. I take out a phone from my floor safe. It's a cell phone I no longer use.

While it powers up, I stroke her everywhere. I already have half a boner when the phone chimes.

Angel tries to grab it from me, but I press the front to my chest. "This is some gruesome shit. Not sure if I should show you. But figure you already guessed some of it." I don't say anything about Mini, and the sense-less violence that killed her. Had nothing to do with the mob, or Angel. Just circumstance. But I'm going to close the circle that I can. Forever.

Her eyes go solemn. "Okay."

"Don't hate me now, Angel."

She shakes her head, catching the side of my face with her cupped hand. "Never."

I hand her the phone.

When she's done scrolling through the pictures, her tears fall off the edge of her chin.

I let my breath out slowly and ask the dreaded question. "Why are you crying?"

Because Jenkins's body in various stages of being beaten and dissolved is pretty fucking disgusting?

"Relief. I'm relieved."

Not what I was expecting. "Oh."

She hands me the phone, and I put it away, using the combination. The airlock sounds, and we look at each other.

Angel moves into my arms. "Happy too."

"Happy I killed him?" I ask softly.

"Happy you made it slow."

She doesn't see my smile.

How doctors can screw up a penis from a vagina is a mystery. All those ultrasounds saying our kid was a boy?

Wrong.

Angel gives me a tired smile.

Hell, I was fucking exhausted after watching her push our daughter out.

I'm so goddamned glad I'm not a woman that I want to celebrate.

Instead, I sit by my wife, so happy I could die, and realize I don't have to. I'm finally living.

The hospital door opens, and Angel's real mom comes in.

They smile at each other. Angel decided it was better to welcome her parent instead of hate her for what neither had control over.

Besides, we named our daughter Beth.

Angel held her mom when she cried after we told her.

Bethany holds her granddaughter now, and Angel cries.

But not because she's sad.

Because she finally isn't.

THE END

Also in paperback:

TRAINER
ROAD KILL MC BOOK 7

Thank you for your attention:

Marata Eros is the pen name for **Tamara Rose Blodgett.**

Love ROAD KILL MC? *Please read on for a sample of another Marata Eros work…*

THE PEARL SAVAGE

A SAVAGE SERIES NOVEL
BOOK 1

New York Times Bestselling Author
TAMARA ROSE BLODGETT

PROLOGUE
1890

Samuel lay on his back, gasping for air like a fish out of the sea. They had done all they could. Now the burden rested with their descendants. His gaze lingered on the house he loved, covered in ash, the sun no longer a bright orb in the sky, but shrouded in gray. A hush fell over the pewter wasteland. Cold seeped into his marrow inch by insidious inch. Many would enter the spheres constructed by the Guardians. Their saviors spoke of selective population, which rang false to Samuel, or true, as the case might be. His grandchildren were safe and beyond the pale of this time, this world he was leaving.

He let his head roll limply on its side, where his gaze captured Mae, also prone with a strange contraption with hand-hammered copper and a complex, inky black netting covering the greater part of her nose and mouth. Leather straps braided and wrapped her skull, pushing strands of hair around like lost silver. She made odd, whistling noises as she breathed.

"Samuel, wear it." Mae's voice was distorted as she lifted the matching mask the Guardians had fashioned in the preceding months.

"No, Mae. I wish to enjoy this fore-night without the chains of their advances."

Samuel knew his stubbornness would cost him his life. The Guardians, who were equal part savior and bearer of terrible news, had made concessions for the elders. But those who survived would be the strongest, most virile, agile, and smartest among them. Samuel and Mae both understood at their advanced age of sixty and one years that they would be excluded from the mercies of the sphere.

With blurred vision, Samuel saw a familiar figure approach.

"Father! Why do you not take rest in your own bed?" Stella's comely face was a salve in his approaching death. Her wool skirts swirled as she knelt and set an illuminated candle, hissing steam from its seams, beside him.

Raising his hand, he cupped the loveliness of her face, knowing the time had come for her to enter the sphere the Guardians had constructed for the *select*. Her eyes brimmed with tears. "Papa, the Guardians have told you that you might survive... All is not lost."

Samuel put a finger to her lips. "Silence now, child. This is your place now. Do not forget the things you have been taught. Take this, Dear Heart. Hold it safe to your breast. Guard it. It is our history." Samuel handed her a slim leather book bound with a black silk tie. Stella pressed it to her chest, tears overflowing down unprotected cheeks. Mae's eyes met hers. "Go now, Stella-girl. Take the opportunity you have been given."

Her knuckles whitened as Stella clutched the book. Misery etched its path on her countenance. "It will never be the same without you both."

A clear bell-tone pealed, reminding Stella of duty, her duty to leave her parents behind. The knowledge of her future, the safe environment of the sphere, was a burden on her heart.

Stella turned to look at the sphere shimmering in a watery iridescence like a giant cloche. But people were not plants. Their future safekeeping was a promise of a life with a family fractured by separation.

Stella bent to kiss Samuel and Mae goodbye. Gently unwinding the facemask the Guardians had constructed, she placed a kiss, soft as butterfly wings on the woman who had nurtured her. The skin gave way like tissue-thin silk under the pressure of her lips. Turning to her father, she saw his pale blue eyes watering. She cradled his head while she pressed a kiss to his forehead. She lowered his head and took a last lingering look, knowing this was the final time she would view her parents in this realm.

Lifting her skirts, she pivoted away, dropping them as she walked—no, as she ran—brushing tears from her cheeks, the book clutched tightly in her other hand, the candle hanging from its copper loop in her squeezed finger. Approaching the doorway to the sphere, she was the last *select* to be ushered inside. Casting one final glance, she saw her parents' supine forms, their clasped hands held tightly, her mother's mask forgotten beside her.

Stella whirled toward the entrance, losing hold of the book, dropping it on the ash-laden earth. She picked it up, her last gift from Father. Seeing the title, she peered closer: *Asteroid: A History of When the Rocks Fell.*

Stella moved forward as the hole closed behind her. A fierce idea bloomed in her consciousness to remember who they had been. An indeterminate future stretched before her.

1

ONE HUNDRED FORTY YEARS LATER

Clara beheld the shrouded exterior as she did each morning, her hands pressed against the pliable interior of the sphere. Her fingers sank into its surface, stopped before breaching the Outside. The yearning was the same. She wished to experience the Outside.

Sighing, Clara turned from the misty view outside the molded window. Her petticoats swept together, wrapping her bare legs, as she found the stockings laid out for her on the bed.

Olive knocked on the door. "Mistress, may I enter your chamber?"

"Yes."

She entered with scads of rich turquoise steam-pressed clothing draped over her arm. Clara hated it, hated it all.

"Princess." Olive inclined her head.

Clara recognized she was penalizing Olive unfairly. Who truly wished to celebrate her Day of Birth? Utter nonsense.

Olive peered at her Princess from under her lashes. She was a formidable young lady with aquamarine eyes that flashed with energetic temper, deep mahogany hair cascading to her waist—very handsome but uncooperative when it came to dressing.

"Please, Princess, they await your appearance."

"Does my mother?"

Olive knew that the Queen was deep in her cup, and it was not yet midday. "Our Queen has begun her own celebration."

No surprise.

Clara's people wished to see her adorned in her finery (a loathsome pursuit) to be reminded that she was their Princess, the one who saw to their happiness, unlike her mother, the Queen, who failed them at every turn.

Olive interrupted her musings. "My lady, please employ the bedpost."

Grabbing the stays that bound the corset, Olive took up the slack. Reaching the end, she pulled with all her might. Clara gasped. "Must it be so tight? I cannot breathe properly."

"It must be hand-span."

Finally, Olive bent to use the shoe hook on Clara's high heels, each button a luminescent mother-of-pearl.

"Do you not think you are agreeable, mistress?"

Clara gazed at her image. Creamy expanses of pale skin met the weak light from the sphere window climbing up to a heart-shaped face with high cheekbones and strange-colored blue eyes, a dark fall of hair that was fiery red in a certain light, brushed her hips where they swelled. Her mother would be pleased, she supposed. But Clara wanted to change into the waistcoat and linen skirt she wore when she visited the oyster fields.

She turned to Olive. "I look comely enough to satisfy the Queen."

"And Prince Frederick."

Yes, she must not forget her upcoming nuptials to the Prince. The thought brought a searing tide of resentment, coiling painfully under her breastbone.

Clara sat at the vanity while Olive wove pearls into her hair. A rainbow of shimmering colors winked in the plaiting. "Do you wish to wear it all up, your highness?" She indicated the back of Clara's head.

She wished to not attend her Day of Birth celebration.

"No, Olive, just the forward section... leave the remainder down."

Olive swept the forward part of Clara's hair off her face in an elaborate coil, twining at the top, back of her head and weaving around it like a crown. Then arranged and rearranged Clara's hair until she was satisfied.

"There. That will do," she said with satisfaction.

Clara stared at her reflection. He eyes gazed back, huge in her small face. Pearls shimmered in the low light.

She stood, giving Olive a gracious nod. "You are most clever with your ministrations."

Olive gave Clara a deep curtsey, which she bore as she did her other royal obligations.

Clara wandered over to her window again, pressing her face almost to the sphere barrier, its soft but impenetrable surface her prison.

"Princess?"

"Yes, Olive," Clara said without turning.

"I implore you. Do not stand so close to the window. You have heard the reports of *savages,* have you not?"

Yes, she had. Again Clara thought of how she longed to explore, to see for herself what lay beyond her world, the Kingdom of Ohio.

"Yes, I have heard and it aggrieves me mightily. If some have survived the bounds of this place," Clara stretched out her hand to encompass the sphere, "who are we to feel disinclination? Should we not welcome others?"

"It is not safe, my Princess."

"And who has such musings?"

"The Record Keeper, my lady."

Clara's full lips thinned into a line of distaste. She detested the idea that one individual held the history and direction of so many.

"Please... make my excuses for another half hour hence."

Olive hesitated, thinking of the Queen's displeasure. "Yes, Princess."

"You are not to be blamed. Tell the Queen that I was obstinate, as is typical." Clara's mouth curved into a smile. It pleased her that Queen Ada would suffer irritation and keep the dreadful Prince Frederick waiting. A bigger pompous ass the spheres had never seen.

Clara turned to face Outside again. Olive slipped out the door and closed it quietly behind her. Tension slipped out of Clara's shoulders. She felt relieved to own another moment of time before the abhorrent celebration began.

She stood watching the wind (as she had been told that was what it was), caressing the Forest of Trees. As she turned away, she saw movement. She pressed her face to the sphere's interior, her nose pushing in the softness. Outside her window, a great male stood, partially obscured by trees. On his face lay a fierceness. Arrows were slung over a shoulder corded with muscle. He had a bow in one hand and strange clothing covering only part of his body. A shocking expanse of skin showed.

He was fascinating and most assuredly a *savage*.

Without warning, he flew the stand of trees that Clara had been admiring since her childhood, rushing straight for the window she leaned against. Clara clenched her teeth, holding her position, knowing that the sphere was impenetrable, but stale fear flooded her mouth as she watched the huge male advance at an incredible speed. Clara's heart thumped painfully in her chest. When a hair's breadth remained between the sphere and Clara, he stopped.

Bracus looked at the female behind the sphere that the Evil Ones had constructed in his grandfather's grandfather's time. He had watched the female for months and had seen her supervising workers in the fields of sea creatures that yielded shimmering jewels.

He also knew she was beautiful. He wanted her.

She was unlike any of the females he had seen. In his clan, females were rare, highly prized, and safeguarded. His eyes caressed her face, the skin like cream from the cow, her eyes like the sea near his cousin's clan, hair the color of fire burnt down to embers. Bracus looked around warily, knowing he must leave. He was too exposed without the trees at his back. He gave a last look at the female. Her expression seemed indecipherable. He felt vulnerable that he had revealed himself after his careful months of hiding. Turning, he climbed up the hill toward the stand of trees, his long and powerful strides eating up the ground. Reaching the forest, he looked back at the window where the female watched him. He turned back toward the clan.

Clara released the breath she'd been holding, letting it out in a rush. Light-headed, she sat on the fainting couch and put her head between her knees. Between the strange episode with the *savage* and the absurd corset, she could not regain her breath. This is how Olive came upon her when she returned to escort her to the celebration.

Olive rushed to her. "Princess, what ails you?"

Although not her favorite transgression, it was effective, and she lied smoothly to Olive. "I think my stays may need loosening."

"Oh! For the love of the Guardian! Please... forgive me." Olive rushed around to loosen the corset, but Clara knew that would just lengthen the horror of the event and incur additional wrath from the Queen.

"Never mind. It matters not, Olive... hand-span it shall be."

"As you wish, Princess."

As she walked to the doorway, she turned, giving one look back to the window, where the *savage* had looked at her so intimately. He had been so alive, so vital. She knew one thing she had seen would distract her during the entire celebration.

The *savage* had gills.

Clara made her way to the door, swinging it open to the hallway which led to the Gathering Room, a place of joy. But not for her... not today.

2

Clara entered with Olive, her lady-in-waiting, who she also called friend, at her heels. Royalty was a lonely role and every friendship sacred. Clara searched the crowd for Charles. Surely he was somewhere around the room. *Nowhere... drat.*

Her eyes scanned the Gathering Room, taking in the rich tapestries lining the walls. "Walls" was a misnomer. There was no puncturing the interior of the sphere. The tapestries had been hung from scaffolding with copper fasteners. The huge Gathering clock *donged*, chiming three hours past noon. Clara loved the enormous time-piece. Ten feet in diameter, it had a symmetry that gave one pause, its beauty striking as sure as the chime she felt reverberating in her chest. The steam-powered gears moved and clanked, clearly seen through a layer of crystal. Hot vapors rose to the highest apex of the sphere, flowing through unseen air portals, which fed to a central ventilator.

Relief swept through Clara as she saw Charles moving toward her. He had finished his studies one year ago and begun to work in the fields. He would stay by her, understanding that she would have to spend a good portion of her time in the presence of her betrothed.

She noticed that he wore his clothes with grace and charm. He looked dashing, his hat a shining wonder topping soft black hair, his time piece tucked safely in the front pocket of a smartly striped brocade vest. His soft velvet pants were charcoal, tucked into tall boots that rose to the knee. His deep black coat lined in scarlet swirled mid-thigh.

Charles bowed. "Princess Clara." His eyes twinkled. The sod knew very well how she hated the title.

Clara automatically returned a perfunctory curtsy. "I see you are in good spirits."

"Ah yes, a Day of Birth celebration for my dearest friend, what must I feel badly about?" Charles raised a brow, tapping a finger on his head as if confused.

Olive giggled behind them. She found Charles amusing. Clara did as well, but not so much this day.

Charles examined her expression. "Clara." He lowered his voice. "There is no alternative. You must persevere."

His sadness cloaked her. Charles would rather slay himself with his own sword than have her married to Frederick.

Clara felt shame redden her cheeks. He was her dear friend and as constrained by rules as she. Taking his hand, she squeezed it, and he leaned down, whispering in her ear, "That is the Clara I know, brave heart. Take my arm, Princess."

Clara slipped her arm through Charles's, noticing how tall he had become. The top of her head brushed his chin. His dark eyes regarded her solemnly. It was time to greet Queen Ada, her mother.

They approached the throne upon its circular dais. The steps leading to her throne shone in the warm light of the steam-chandeliers, their crystal orbs casting a golden glow directly over the dais, spreading like molten water over the floor.

The Queen regarded them with thinly veiled disdain, her tapered finger eternally running up and down the crystal stem of her shimmering emerald wine goblet.

"Daughter of mine," Queen Ada said with silken menace encasing every syllable, "what reason have you for being late to your own Day of Birth celebration? Leaving"—she gave a slight incline of her head—"Prince Frederick in a most unescorted plight." Her gaze bored through Clara.

She allowed herself to look at Prince Frederick, whose thunderous expression told her that her mother was not the only one from whom she would have to assuage temper.

"Do not look at Prince Frederick," Queen Ada roared, causing the crowd to gasp. "Address your Queen!"

Charles moved behind Clara, putting his hand at the small of her back.

Queen Ada's razor stare turned to Charles. "She is not to be coddled."

Charles hand fell away from Clara's back, and she stood, vulnerable and seemingly alone, before Ada.

Clara took a stoic breath, bracing herself, knowing the shock wave she would send through the crowd. "I have a tale of great magnitude." Every eye was upon Clara. A feeling of great excitement stole around her heart, squeezing it. "I have seen a *savage*."

The gasps were as one, loud in their combined softness.

Queen Ada stood, her goblet temporarily forgotten. Elvira, her lady-in-waiting, swooped forward to steady it. Clara watched Ada regain her balance, swaying only a little.

"You lie." She stood in her swirling gown of deep purple, her favorite color, with a long, sensuous rope of black pearls looped and knotted, reaching her knees. Samuel's pearls, only the rarest for Ada. Clara never thought of her mother as such. It was always Ada, or the Queen.

"I do not. I was taking my leave before this celebration." Clara turned to the many faces, some of which she was close enough to reach out and touch, and spoke to them, giving her back to Ada, a brave thing. "I saw him at the border of the Forest, which lays Outside."

More gasping. The sightings of the *savages* had increased in number, along with the sentries at the critical sphere passages between kingdoms.

Charles grasped her elbows, turning her to face him. "You say you saw one? How close, *Cla*... Princess."

"I ask the questions here, not you." The Queen turned her fearsome expression to Clara. "Perchance, you use this ridiculous story as a ruse to win you my mercy for the disrespect you show us by your lateness." She looked at Clara, for all her drink, brightly and with a keenness that Clara knew very well.

Clara ignored the question, hoping to distract with her tale.

"He ran with great speed to my window." Many voices began at once, and Clara was forced to stop.

"Silence!" Queen Ada bellowed, and the crowd's voices faded.

Ada swung her attention to Frederick. "What say you? Does my daughter bear tales?"

As if he would have a fig's reckoning about her state of mind.

Frederick glared down at Clara. She a terrible but necessary inconvenience, one he would obtain to further his wealth. She was but a pawn on his kingdom's chessboard.

Frederick sat slightly lower and to the left of Ada, the King of Kentucky to Ada's right. It was he, not Frederick, who answered. "If I may, I feel disinclined that Princess

Clara would falsify such a tale at a time when these *savages* are unveiling their presence."

Clara gulped back her anxiety, eternally thankful for King Otto, who inadvertently paved the way for her next comment. "I may know why they survive Outside." The silence was that of a tomb, but Clara continued. "The male had..." Clara gestured to the slender column of her neck, and the many faces of the crowd followed her motion. "...gills. They appear to aid in his breathing."

Excited conversations exploded all around Clara, and she hazarded a look at Queen Ada, who looked as if her breath had been stolen, sitting down in a very un-royal heap upon her throne.

Charles studied Clara, his hand still encircling an elbow when Prince Frederick was suddenly there. "Unhand my betrothed, Mr. Pierce."

Charles stared at the Prince with an unwavering gaze, his brown eyes steady, his fingers loosening then falling away. Clara looked at Charles, her eyes warning him. She saw in his eyes a wish to maim, which would not do. It would not do at all. Her gaze traveled, finding the Prince's guards.

"Come, Clara." He said her name with an intimacy he would never earn. "Sit beside your future king."

Clara would rather drown in the oyster fields than be near him. She turned to look at Charles, and he mouthed, *I will be here.*

Clara lifted her skirts to assure her footing as she climbed the dais and sat in the small, gilded throne at Ada's left, sandwiched between the loathsome Prince and her drunken mother, the one who would prostitute her for free grapes, giving up their precious legacy of pearls for her love of the cup.

3

Clara's gaze fell upon the crowd, so deeply engaged in the titillating news of a close sighting of a *savage*. Not a glimpse, no, but an entirely intimate appraisal. She felt the uncomfortable presence of Prince Frederick at her back. He had made it clear that she was not suitable for him. With her very unfeminine desire to work the oyster fields, he had been quite vocal in his dislike of her duties.

His irritation pleased her.

It was well known, at least in her sphere, that the Kingdom of Kentucky was ill managed. Prince Frederick acted not in the least concerned for his people's prosperity. There had been rumors of poverty, which included starvation, unheard of in most spheres.

A hand gripped her collarbone painfully, and Clara checked her expression so the pain would not show.

"Smile, my dear, let them all know how happy you are that I have deigned to show my affection for you," the Prince whispered, his breath so like rotten fruit that Clara stifled a gag. She plastered a false smile on her face, which immediately alarmed Charles. Clara gave a minute shake of her head, *stay there,* the look said. She was stuck as a butterfly with a pin through its wing. The Prince abused her in a multitude of subtleties. She could guess what a marriage with him would entail. He released her, and the numbness where his hand had been faded, replaced with throbbing that kept pace with her heart.

Ada leaned forward. "You will explain this later, my daughter. In detail."

"Yes, my Queen."

Ada placed her hand at the back of Clara's neck and squeezed hard, her favorite tender spot to abuse. At every vantage point, she was higher than Clara, as tall as most men, and always higher on the dais, *always.* Clara struggled not to whimper at the double abuse from the Prince and the Queen. It was a near thing and difficult to hide from her people.

Ada and King Otto had their heads pressed together in royal commune, which suited Clara very well. It meant that the Queen's attention lay elsewhere. Finally, amongst the noise of the people's conversation, King Otto clapped his hands three times, causing Clara to flinch, which amused Frederick. The crowd quieted.

"Hail the People of the Kingdom of Ohio. On this day, it is not just a Day of Birth Celebration, but also a day of exciting news." A somber expression rode his face. "Your Princess claims to have seen one of these *savages* near at hand and will now explain them to us."

Once more, all eyes were on Clara. As unprepared as she felt, she knew the violence that would meet non-compliance, so she began. "He seemed of rugged countenance but not a danger."

A person from the crowd shouted, "How can that be? We know they are to be feared."

Clara's eyes narrowed, taking in the speaker's stance.

"That is what we have been told by the Record Keeper." A disquieted silence fell. "And this may be, but this *savage* offered no violence. It is my belief that he was... curious about us."

"About *you,* Princess." This came from one of the men who captained the pungy boat in the oyster fields.

"Mayhap of me, or it could be happenstance that I stood by the window at just the right moment."

Olive spoke next. "Tell us, your highness, what did it look like?"

The group leaned forward to catch her words. "He was of huge body and limb, with long hair to here," Clara indicated her shoulders, "and of fierce expression." Clara did not indicate clothing, as it would be an embarrassment in front of the People, his nakedness scandalous.

The great timepiece chimed four times, its deep timber reverberating inside the Gathering Room like a quaking of the earth. Steam rose to the sphere's apex, the hissing vapors seemingly disappearing.

The Queen broke through the questions with a final, "Enough of the supposed *savage*. Let us celebrate my daughter's Day of Birth."

Clara knew Queen Ada wished to know everything in private, an interrogation she would not escape.

Servants came forward with laden plates of grapes, cheese, and all matter of meats and pastries for the last course. A great cake was piled four tiers high. It was an absurd extravagance, more appropriate for a Wedded Joining than a birthday. They laid the feast at the foot of the royal dais on tables that had been arranged for the buffet. Another table was piled high with lavishly packaged gifts from her people.

Clara stood on feet shaky from stress. "Thank you all most kindly for your presence at my Day of Birth Celebration. I am most grateful for your allegiance and loyalty."

Ada waved her hand dismissively. "Yes, *yes* Princess Clara, they understand that." Her eyes narrowed.

Clara thought that might be the case but felt the words were most important to say. The Queen cared not, but Clara knew loyalty was an uncertain thing, cultivated through decent treatment, not fear. A lesson her mother did not ascribe to. A lesson taught by her father, King Raymond, long-since passed.

Someone she would never forgot.

Also available in paperback

ACKNOWLEDGMENTS

I published **The Druid** and **Death Series** in 2011 with the encouragement of my husband, and continued because of you, my Reader. Your faithfulness through comments, suggestions, spreading the word and ultimately purchasing my work with your hard-earned money gave me the incentive, means and inspiration to continue.

There are no words that are sufficiently adequate to express my thankfulness for your support. But know this: TDS novellas continued past HARVEST only because of you.

I truly feel connected to my readers. It is obvious to me, but I'll say the words anyway for clarity: a written work is just words on pages if they are not read by my readers. As I write this I get a lump in my throat; your enjoyment of my work affects me that deeply.

You guys are the greatest, each and every one of ya~

Marata (Tamara) xo

Special Thanks:
You, my reader.
Hubs, who is my biggest fan.
Cameren, without whom, there would be no books.

ABOUT THE AUTHOR

 **Tamara Rose Blodgett**: happily married mother of four sons. Dark fiction writer. Reader. Dreamer. Home restoration slave. Tie dye zealot. Coffee addict. Bead Slut. Digs music.

She is also the *New York Times* Bestselling author of ***A Terrible Love,*** written under the pen name, **Marata Eros,** and over ninety-five other titles, to include the #1 international bestselling erotic Interracial/African-American **TOKEN** serial and her #1 Amazon bestselling Dark Fantasy novel, ***Death Whispers***. Tamara writes a variety of dark fiction in the genres of erotica, fantasy, horror, romance, sci-fi and suspense. She lives in the midwest with her family and three, disrespectful dogs.

Connect with Tamara:

www.tamararoseblodgett.com
Win **FREE** stuff!

Made in the USA
Monee, IL
20 June 2020